What Price Ambition

By

DD Hall

Publisher – D. Skinner
Glenluce, Scotland.
ddhall.author@gmail.com

What Price Ambition?

What Price Ambition is the copyright of Dorothy Skinner
First edition 2018

What Price Ambition?

Chapter I.

The Key.

Anna watched from the window as the young man got out of his sports car, and slung the jacket of his immaculate designer suit over his shoulder, She smiled with satisfaction when he paused before he rang the doorbell, and slipped on the jacket and straightened his tie,
"Yes, you'll do, my Toni," she said softly, "You respect your Nonna."
She waited the five minutes it took him to pass the time of day with the man who let him in, and bound up the stairs two at a time to the sitting room overlooking the gardens. She heard him knock confidently and enter the room,
"Antonio," she said fondly, "Give your Nonna a kiss. How's your mother today?"
"Nonna," said the young man with genuine smile lighting up his slim features, "Mum's fine. She thinks it's just a touch of flu. You look younger every day."

What Price Ambition?

Anna laughed, "And you grow more handsome, Antonio, I expect the girls are queuing up to go out with you."

Antonio grinned, "One or two, Nonna, but nothing serious. You know how it is."

Antonio sat down opposite his Grandmother. He could talk frankly to her about any topic. She was never embarrassed either by his questioning mind, or his open appraisement of life's opportunities,

"Yes, my boy, I know how it is for young men, but be careful, Toni. You see that you choose the right girls, and I hope you take precautions. You don't want to get sick."

"Nonna!" laughed Antonio, "I never said I sleep with them."

"You have your Grandfather's blood." she said and shrugged. Then she leaned forward and took his hand.

"Antonio, you will be twenty one next week. I asked you to come and see me today when your Grandfather is out. I want to talk to you, but I need your word that you will not repeat any of what I'm going to say to anyone. It's to be our secret. Do you promise, Antonio? Swear on the Family's blood."

"Nonna what is this? Of course I promise." he said somberly when he saw the glint in her eyes, "My lips are sealed."

What Price Ambition?

"Good boy. Now, bring me the decanter and two glasses, and pour us some wine while we talk. Have you eaten?"

"Yes thanks. Mum insists we all eat together on Sunday, you know that."

"Of course, and your mother is right. Sundays are for family matters. Come and sit next to me. Pull up that stool."

Antonio handed Anna one of the crystal glasses, and settled down beside her chair with the other between his hands. He looked at the bright, deep ruby richness of the wine brought back from Tuscany by his Grandfather.

"This is good, Nonna. Is this one of Grandpa's investments?"

"Yes, he owns the vineyard. You must go there and see it, Antonio. You would like Tuscany. Perhaps we could go together in the spring."

Antonio smiled, "They'll think you've got a gigolo, Nonna." Anna laughed, "I wish. No, I'm afraid the days when young men turned their heads to look at me are over. Even your Grandfather is more interested in his golf than me."

"He must be blind or getting too old. We'll just have to find you an Italian Romeo, Nonna."

Anna laughed and touched his cheek.

"You're such a joy to me, Antonio. You're my favourite, you know."

What Price Ambition?

"Nonna you're not supposed to have favourites," laughed Antonio, "But, yes, I do know, and I love you."

"Do you know why, Antonio?" and the boy shook his head, "Because you're so like your father. He was my favourite too." she said with a faraway look in her eyes.

"Because he was the eldest, the first born?"

Anna shook her head, "No, it wasn't that. Some day I might tell you, but right now I can't. Antonio, I want to give you something when you're twenty one. It's for you alone. The others must not know."

"Okay, Nonna what is it?"

Anna frowned. Her four children had given her nine grandchildren. Antonio was only the third oldest, but as she had said, he was her favourite. His father was her first-born, but he had married later than his two sisters and had only had one child.

Anna reached for a box on the small table by her chair, and took out an object.

"It's a key, Antonio," she said, and placed the heavy brass key in his hands.

Antonio looked up at her with growing curiosity, "What does it unlock, Nonna?"

"All in good time, my boy," she said mysteriously, "I just want you to keep this key in a safe place till you're called upon to use it, I can't say when that will be, Antonio. It might even be after I'm dead and gone."

"Nonna, you're never going to die."

What Price Ambition?

Anna shook her head sadly, "Oh yes I will, Toni," she whispered, "None of us can escape death."

Antonio gripped both her hands. "But not for a long time yet." he said urgently.

"Well, let's hope not. I want you to make me a solemn promise here today, Antonio," she went on, "I want your word that when you're called upon to unlock the door with this key, you will take up the pledge you will find inside. Do you promise me, Antonio?"

Antonio looked at his Grandmother's faded brown eyes and he saw an intensity in their depth asking for his help. *His* help, no-one else would do, he knew that, although he had no idea why.

"Of course I will, Nonna. I promise on my father's life that I will be your champion whatever the cause is."

"Good boy, Antonio," said Anna and she hugged him, "A toast, Antonio. "To lovers everywhere."

Antonio looked strangely at her, but he raised his glass and repeated her words without comment, knowing that one day he would know their meaning.

"Now, Antonio, tell me what you plan to do with your life," said Anna and she settled back in the armchair.

Antonio sipped his wine, and then he looked straight at his Grandmother.

"I'm going to be very rich, Nonna," he said with such vehemence that Anna smiled.

"And what exactly do you mean by that? Your father, Giorgio, isn't poor, and you will one day inherit his

fortune. He's done well. There aren't many young men your age who have a sports car like that one," she nodded
toward the window.

Antonio grinned, "No, I suppose not. It pulls the girls too," he laughed, "But I have a dream, Nonna. I'm going to race cars."

"No Antonio," said Anna with a start, "That's dangerous."

Antonio laughed again, "I didn't mean drive the car myself. I'm going to build a racing team. We'll win on every circuit. I have this idea, but first I have to earn enough to fund it. Racing isn't cheap. You know my friend Rick and I have a workshop at Dad's factory. We've already modified a formula three car for another friend, Drew Mitchell. You know, the transport people."

Anna nodded, "Yes, your Grandfather and his Grandfather grew up together."

She laughed, "Do you know, when they were boys in Sicily they ran a business selling firewood to the villagers. Everyone had an open fire in those days, the only thing was they used to sell the same bag more than once if they could get away with it. Some folk never checked that they were getting full measure."

"That's dishonest," laughed Antonio, "I never thought Grandpa was like that."

What Price Ambition?

"You don't know your Grandpa at all. He can be a ruthless man when he wants,"
Antonio saw her brow crease, and her eyes take on a gleam which seemed to open a spotlight deep into her soul.
"Anyway, Drew is winning with my modification, and we're going to patent it. It could have far reaching markets in ordinary cars too."
"And what would you need to finance its development, Antonio?" said Anna casually.
"A lot of money, Nonna, and that's why I've got to get into something where I can earn big money quickly."
"And have you any idea what that might be? I know your father was hoping you would change your mind about going to university."
Antonio shook his head, "No, that's a waste of time. I haven't got that long. I've got a good grounding in banking under my belt but there's no money in that side of the business. I'm going into the money market. I want to be a
A Trader in Investment Banking. That's where the big money is."
Have you spoken to your Aunt Sofia. Vittorio's brother is in finance. He might be able to help."
Antonio looked at his Grandmother in surprise, "I didn't know. Thanks, Nonna. I'll speak to Uncle Vittorio. Dad gave me some money to invest when I turned eighteen, He said if I could at least double it by the time I was

twenty one, he would finance a small business for me. I've trebled it Nonna, and I'm going to present the figures to him on my birthday. You are coming aren't you?"

"I wouldn't miss it and I want the first dance, My Toni. Come and give your Nonna a hug, and then get my jacket. We're going for a spin in that car of yours. Down to the coast, I think."

Antonio laughed, "Why don't you get one for yourself, Nonna?"

"Oh no," said Anna with a mischievous smile, "It's not half as much fun as being driven by my favourite Grandson. We can drive along the beach road. All the girls will be green with envy."

After their drive, Anna kissed his cheek as he got back in the driver's seat.

"A perfect day, Antonio. You're the only one who thinks about your Grandmother. The only one who doesn't mind spending time with me. Antonio, you know that your Grandfather, Mario, is the Don for this family. Has your

father spoken to you about it?"

"No Nonna, he hasn't, but Mum told me that one day Dad will take over from Grandpa."

Anna squeezed Antonio's hand, "Your father doesn't want that responsibility. He has never been interested. Do you know what that means, Antonio?"

Antonio shook his head again,

What Price Ambition?

"It means that your Grandfather will have to find another head for the Family.
He should nominate your father's brother, your Uncle Sergio. Sergio will be Don and you will lose your birthright. Antonio, I won't let that happen again."
He saw her mouth tighten at the corners.
Antonio looked at her closely, "What do you mean, Nonna?"
"It's your birthright, Antonio, twice over. The head of the Family is yours, and I will see that you get it. Now go home, and take your mother some of this tonic. The pharmacist makes it up for me."
Antonio got in his car and waved to his grandmother as he drove towards the gates at the end of the driveway, but he was so engrossed in what she had said that he did not see the girl step of the pavement in front of him.
Suddenly she was there, her hands on the bonnet of the car, her face staring through the windscreen at him in horror. He thumped his foot on the brake, and the car stopped with a screech, and slid on the gravel. Fortunately, he had not been going at any speed, but even so, the momentum of the car carried the girl forward two or three feet.
Antonio threw open the door and jumped out. He ran round the bonnet to her, and saw that she was slumped against the headlights on the nearside, her eyes closed and her hands gripping the bumper. Antonio saw her breasts heave under the tight fitting sweater she wore,

and he stared as the swell pushed the fabric provocatively. Her black tights were ripped, and he stared at that too.

The run in them went all the way up her thigh where he caught a glimpse of buttock revealed when her short skirt had ridden up on impact with the car.

His grandmother's shouts of concern brought him to his senses, and he took the girl's arm.

"Are you alright?" he asked anxiously, "I didn't see you step off the pavement, I'm sorry, It was my fault."

"Mama mia, Antonio, is she injured?" said Anna, "Shall I get an ambulance?"

The girl brushed her short hair from her face and smiled weakly,

"No, I'm alright, Mrs. Agusto. Really, I'm just shaken. I'll be alright when I get home. I live just there, next door." she explained to Antonio, "And it was my fault, I didn't look. I was thinking about something. There's no harm done. Really."

"Well if you're sure," said Antonio, "Here, let me at least help you to your door." he added as she tried to put her weight on her leg.

"I think I've twisted it," she said, "Thanks. If I could just take your arm."

Antonio grinned,, "I can do better than that," he said with a laugh, and swept her off her feet into his arms.

Antonio played rugby, and trained regularly at the local gym, and she weighed hardly anything. He ignored her protest, and strode down the path to her front door where he set her down carefully.

"The least I can do for a damsel in distress," he laughed, "I'm Antonio Agusto, her grandson." he said nodding towards his Grandmother who had gone back inside the house.

"Beccy Roberts," the girl said, "You're Italian, aren't you?"

"No, I was born right here in Glasgow, but Nonna and Grandpa came from Italy. He was a prisoner of war here in Scotland during the last war and he decided to settle here. He went to Italy to marry my Grandmother, and he brought her back here.

"They have an ice cream business, don't they?" said Beccy, "Mum says it's the biggest in Scotland."

Antonio grinned, "Yes, she's probably right. Look, shouldn't you go in and rest that foot."

Beccy smiled, "I suppose so. Thanks for your help."

"My help!" laughed Antonio, "I'm lucky you're not suing me, at least for the price of a pair of tights," he nodded at the ruined hosiery.

Beccy looked down at her legs and she blushed, "Well maybe I should. They cost a fortune."

"How about dinner?" said Antonio, and Beccy looked at him in astonishment.

"Dinner," he repeated, "You know, where two people sit down and eat together."

What Price Ambition?

"I'm sorry," said Beccy and Antonio saw the pink tinge of embarrassment on her face, "You must think I'm awful silly. no-one's ever asked me out to dinner before. The boys I meet don't do that sort of thing."
"Then you're not meeting the right guys. I'll pick you up at seven tomorrow."
"Okay, thanks. That will be nice. I'll see you tomorrow."
She opened the door and went inside and Antonio grinned as he turned and walked back to his car.
Beccy was pretty with short blonde hair and blue eyes
"Innocent as a baby," he said out loud to himself, "This could be interesting."
He conjured up an image of her in his mind. Her shapely legs, and the glimpse of the trim buttock. The swell of her breasts pressing against the tight sweater as if trying to escape. He was not sure if he would enjoy her company.
He did not like to have to try too hard with a girl, and he usually went for the ones who knew the score. Beccy would be different, a challenge. She had never been out to dinner. Maybe there were other things she had never experienced. He could teach her, mould her to his liking. He was suddenly looking forward to it.
Antonio had left school at eighteen with good exam results, and had got a job with the bank where the family business held it's account. His parents wanted

him to go to university, but he had other plans. However, he did
condescend to go to college in his own time to augment his qualifications. He had no doubt that he would succeed, and it never crossed his mind for one moment that he would ever become one of the statistics on the unemployment register when he left school. He would be successful. The alternative was not an option for him.

In a way, he was right, for his Grandmother was at that very moment sowing the seeds for him.

Her husband, Antonio's grandfather, had arrived home, and she spoke to him immediately he had settled in his armchair.

"Don't you dare fall asleep, old man," she commanded, "I want to talk to you."

"What is it now, Anna?" said Mario Agusta, "I've had a strenuous day, and I just want a few minutes peace and quiet."

"You've only been playing golf, and probably propping up the bar for most of it," retorted Anna, "Now, just you listen to me, Mario Agusta. Our grandson, Antonio needs our help,"

Mario waved his hand, "Rubbish, woman. His father takes care of Antonio's needs. Giorgio has done well for himself,"

"Yes, he has," agreed Anna, "But Antonio needs help from you, Mario. I want you to make sure he gets a good job, Find out what the boy wants to do, and get someone to make him an offer. Call in a few debts."

Mario looked at his wife steadily, "That's not for you to dictate, Anna." He said quietly,

Anna stood in front of him defiantly.

"Mario Agusta, I want this for my Grandson. Do you hear? If you won't do it there are others who will."

Mario looked at her coldly, and Anna shivered involuntarily, but she kept up her steady gaze till he nodded slowly.

"Alright, this one time for you, Anna," he said slowly, "My god, woman, you try my patience sometimes."

"You have no patience, Mario," said Anna, "And there was a time when you needed help."

"That's enough, Anna," said Mario sharply, "You've almost crossed the line, woman."

Anna turned away and went to the door. She knew that Mario was talking about Omerta, the code of silence, and she knew too that she *had* taken her point to the edge.

"I'll wake you in an hour for tea." she said and left him to sleep in his armchair, the matter closed again.

Mario went to see Giorgio next day, and found out what it was Antonio was planning as a career. Within the week, Antonio received a strange phone call from a prestigious firm of bankers asking him what his plans were for the future.

What Price Ambition?

It left him in a good mood when, after work at the bank, he went to see Beccy for the second time.

Their first date had been pleasant. Antonio found to his surprise that she was an interesting person for someone her age with lots of opinions about life, and she was at college doing computer and business studies. He had taken her home quite early, and simply kissed her cheek when he said goodnight at her door. He knew she wanted him to do more, but he felt like stringing her along till the next date. He wanted to savour the anticipation of making love to her

slowly. Not for one second did he consider that she would reject him when he said he would see her the coming Monday.

Beccy did not reject him, and here he was on his way to pick her up.

First, however, he called to see his Grandmother.

"Antonio!" said Anna in surprise, "I was going to phone you later. How did you get on today?"

"Why, is there something I should know" he said with a smile "I had a phone call from someone who knows Grandpa today. I don't suppose he had anything to do with it." he grinned.

"Now, would your Grandpa interfere, Antonio," said Anna with a smile, "You just make the most of the opportunity, my boy."

"I will, Nonna," said Antonio, "And thanks. I'm taking Beccy out." he added.

What Price Ambition?

"The girl next door," said Anna in surprise, "I wouldn't have thought she was your type, Antonio."
"She's not like some of the girls I take out," Antonio admitted, "She's a bit old fashioned really. Believes in romance and principles."
"There's nothing wrong with that, Antonio," said Anna, "She's a nice girl. Thoughtful."
Antonio left his Grandparents' house and went next door. Beccy was ready, and he smiled when she appeared at the door in a short sleeveless dress with a jacket slung over her arm. It was a warm evening,
"You look nice," he said appreciatively, "I thought we could go for something to eat and them a movie, unless you would rather do something else."
Beccy smiled shyly, assuring him that it would be fine, and Antonio knew that she was happy just to be with him whatever he decided to do.
He took her hand as they left the cinema.
"It's a lovely evening," he said, "Let's drive down to the river. Do you fancy a burger. I'm starving."
They bought some food at the van parked nearby, and strolled slowly through the gardens beside the river. Antonio rolled the paper into a ball when he finished eating, and threw it into the bin,
"You're a good shot," Beccy laughed, "You seem to be good at everything you do, Antonio."
He grabbed her hand and pulled her towards him,
"I try." he said and kissed her slowly.

Beccy responded at once, for she had wanted him to kiss her all evening.

Antonio felt her body stir and a heat started to creep through him from the nape of his neck. Her breath was hot and sweet on his face, and he kissed her eyes, and her neck till he found her lips again, His hands felt her body through the thin cotton dress, and his fingers traced the outline of her briefs across her hips before he slid his hands up to her breasts, and squeezed, his fingers gently probing for her nipples. Beccy gasped as he stimulated them to a hardness with his thumb and forefinger through the fabric. She moaned when he pushed her dress up over her hips and slid his fingers inside the tiny briefs she wore till he felt the moistness tease his skin. She kissed him passionately with a sharp intake of breath at the sensuousness of his touch, and she did not protest when he bent her over backwards and laid her on the grass. He started to undo his trousers and fumbled in frustration when the zip got caught. In that second, Beccy was jolted from the trance of the passionate euphoria she was in. She stiffened and pushed him away, feeling the fire in her

body when she felt him push between her legs.

"No, please don't. I don't want to go all the way." she said in a panic.

Antonio was poised over her, and he sank momentarily against her before he jumped to his feet.

"I thought you did," he said, "You didn't stop me."

What Price Ambition?

"I don't mind heavy petting," she said and got up too, "But I don't go all the way."

"And what if I had insisted?" he said with an edge to his voice, for he was strung up, "Some guys would have taken that as an open invitation, and you wouldn't have had any choice. It's dangerous games you're playing, Beccy. I'll take you home."

"Antonio," she called as he turned away, "I'm sorry, I didn't mean to upset you. I don't want to have sex with anyone yet. I want it to be something special. I only let boys touch me because they expect it."

He turned back towards her and put his hands on her shoulders.

"We expect it if you lead us on like that, Beccy. I'm only human, and I'm not a mind reader. You should tell a guy if you don't want to go that far."

She looked at him miserably, "It's not that, Antonio. I *do* want to. I feel, I don't know, I want to make love, but I want it to be special, you know. I want to be in love when I do it."

Antonio smiled, "You're a romantic, Beccy. Too nice for this life, but you'll have to cool it if you want to save yourself for that special guy."

He kissed her gently and held her close.

"When I get wandering palms, you'll have to put the brakes on, for no guy is going to do it for you, least of all me."

What Price Ambition?

She nodded, "I understand. I'm sorry. I think I want to go home now."

Antonio took her home, and he kissed her again on the doorstep

"Goodbye, Antonio," she whispered, "And thanks, I enjoyed going out with you."

"What do you mean, goodbye?" he said in surprise, "I was hoping to see you on Saturday. I'm having a party, It's my birthday."

This time it, was Beccy's turn to sound surprised.

"But I didn't think you'd want to see me again."

Antonio looked at her. How wrong could she be. She fascinated him. Stirred him to almost a frenzy of emotion. He loved her quaint naivety. It was a change from the brash, street-wise girls he usually dated.

"Well you're wrong. I'd like to see you again, Beccy, and I promise I won't come on heavy next time."

Beccy's face radiated with pleasure.

It was my fault. You'll pick me up, will you?"

Antonio grinned, "No, I'll get Nonna to bring you. They're coming to the party too. I have to be there to welcome my guests."

He held her hands for a minute before he left and got in his car, and he waved as he drove off.

The party was a great success with all Antonio's friends and family filling the hotel banqueting suite his father had booked,

What Price Ambition?

"Come on, Nonna, you promised me a dance," he said, and whirled Anna on to the floor, "You dance with Beccy, Grandpa." he called over his shoulder.

"Do you like her, Antonio?"

Antonio moved back from Anna and looked at her.

"She's alright," he said suspiciously, "Now don't you go reading anything in to it, Nonna. I'm not ready for a steady relationship. I've only been out with her twice."

"Tonight is the third time," Anna corrected him, "She likes you, Antonio."

"Don't they all," grinned Antonio with confident charm.

"Your Grandpa has a surprise for you," said Anna changing the subject, "He'll tell you himself later."

Antonio was curious. His Grandfather was a powerful man, and Antonio knew that he could make things happen if he so chose. Antonio had been brought up in the tradition of the Cosa Nostra, established in the City in the late forties when Italian immigrants had stayed on after the war to build businesses in the community. As their wealth increased, hereditary obligations to the organisation which had controlled their ancestors was still a matter of honour. In some cases it was also a matter of debt, for their success was due to the continued interest of the Family.

Mario Agusta had taken control of the family in his area with the blessing of the old Country, and had diligently collected the monies due to him for his continuing benevolence. Everyone had worked hard to make the

What Price Ambition?

business a success, and now that Mario was rich and secure, he could put back some of the wealth he had created into the community which had sustained him. Many a charity and even individuals had benefitted from his generosity, and it was easy for the beneficiaries to ignore the more forceful directions he often issued to his lieutenants.

Business was guarded jealously, and the area strictly divided into operational

sectors, and none of the Dons strayed without very good reason or a sudden wish to die. The Dons were ruthless men when their authority was challenged, and if necessary, enforced their will with violence.

Antonio had never seen any of this, but even as a child at school he had been made aware of his Grandfather's position. To Antonio, Mario was a strict but kind grey-haired man who brought him ice-cream from the factory where he made it. Mario had always supported him in anything he had chosen to do, and Antonio had always had the best that Mario's money could but for him.

It was towards the end of the evening that his Grandfather came to find him.

He had Antonio's father with him, and he smiled as he approached Beccy and Antonio.

"There you are, Antonio," Mario said fondly, "I'm sure Beccy won't mind if I steal you away for a little while. Over here, Duncan." he called to Antonio's cousin,

What Price Ambition?

"Look after this young lady for your cousin, Antonio. I want to talk to him."

Antonio squeezed Beccy's arm, and left her with Duncan while he followed the two older men to a table in the corner.

"More wine," called Mario to a passing waiter, but Antonio shook his head when the waiter poured the wine into the glasses, He had already drank a fair amount and he was light-headed enough. He wanted to know exactly what his Grandfather was saying to him,

The elderly man sat easily in the chair with his elbows on its arms, fingers lightly pressed together, and he looked at Antonio for several seconds before he spoke,

"Antonio, do you know who I am?" Mario asked cryptically, and Antonio looked at him.

"I don't understand," he said with a puzzled frown, "You're my Grandfather."

"Yes, I am, but I'm also the head of the Family here. Do you know what that means, Antonio?"

"The Mafia," said Antonio bluntly, "You're head of the Mafia, Grandpa."

Mario nodded, "You don't think too much of that, I see." Antonio glanced at his father who said nothing.

"I try not to think of it, Grandpa, It's not something I'm proud of. The Mafia conjures up all sorts of nasty images, and people stay clear when they know my connections.

What Price Ambition?

"So, you're ashamed to be associated with the family, my boy," said Mario.
"Not ashamed, Grandpa," said Antonio quickly, "It just doesn't figure in my life."
"Ah, but that's where you're wrong, Antonio. Everything you have is because I as Don have sanctioned it. Tell me, who paid for that flash school you went to, and how did they get that nice sports pavilion? Who financed the
Club you and your friends wanted here? Who made sure your friend's mother wanted for nothing while her husband was in hospital, and who got you out of trouble that time you and your friends stole that car for kicks when you were thirteen? The list is endless, Antonio, The Church, the Businesses, The People in the community. All owe a debt of thanks to the Family."
"I didn't realise, Grandpa, but what about the rest, the pressure to conform and contribute, the dubious business methods, Drugs."
"You've been watching too much television, Antonio," replied Mario without hesitation, "Don't believe everything you see and hear."
"Well, the other stuff then," persisted Antonio, "You've been involved in some violence round here. I'm not stupid, Grandpa, I hear the talk."
"There are some people who just will not honour our code, Antonio," said Mario darkly ."They need to be taught a lesson."

What Price Ambition?

"But torching their homes, Grandpa. That's real barbaric."

"You don't know anything, Antonio." said Mario shortly, "Like I said, you shouldn't believe everything you hear."

"But men were arrested for that, Grandpa," said Antonio, "They say you paid them to take the wrap. You did set them up, didn't you, Grandpa? Don't you feel guilty at all?"

"You don't know what you're saying, my boy," said Mario mildly, "The wine has gone to your head. I didn't do it," he said firmly, which in essence Antonio knew was the truth. "But even if I had, they can't prove anything. There are

some things you have to do as Don which leaves a sour taste in your mouth, as you will find out when it's your turn."

"My turn?" said Antonio, "I don't think so, Grandpa."

Mario smiled, "That saddens me, Antonio. I was hoping that one day you will be Don in my place."

Mario looked at his son, Giorgio, "Your father has renounced the responsibility. I respect his decision, although, I have to say I'm disappointed. Your Uncle

Sergio should be my obvious choice after your father, but I want you to take it on, Antonio, and your sons after you."

What Price Ambition?

Antonio shook his head, "No, Grandpa, I can't. I have plans for my life and it doesn't include being nursemaid to this town."

"Yes, I know. You want to build a winning racing team. Do you know how much money that takes, Antonio?"

"Yes, and I'll get it."

"You would get it quicker if you stayed in the Family. I have another offer for you. You can go and join one of the best banks in the world tomorrow. Go to London. Work with them. Learn the business, make money quickly, Antonio. I've arranged it for you. It's yours for the taking, my boy. All I want is your commitment to take over when the time comes. Your father is happy with that too, isn't that right, Giorgio?"

Antonio's father nodded, "Yes. I haven't the right attitude, Antonio. I wouldn't be any good at it, but you have. I saw it in you even as a boy. You can be Don if you want to, but I'm not putting any pressure on you."

Antonio brushed his fingers through his short, spiked hair, and poured himself some wine while he mulled over his Grandfather's offer.

"I don't know. I would like to think I can do it on my own, but it's tempting, Grandpa. In five years I could be in production with a new car, and on the circuits in seven. Ten years could win me the world championship with

the right driver."

What Price Ambition?

Mario smiled, "Big ambitions, my boy. Think about it, and by the way, I've got tickets for the Grand Prix next month. You and I will go. I want you to meet the men who matter in the racing world."

Antonio laughed, "That's an offer I can't refuse, Grandpa. Okay, you have my commitment."

Antonio stood up and held out his hand to his Grandfather and Mario gripped it firmly.

Antonio bowed his head slightly, "Don Mario, you have my word. The Family is my commitment."

"You won't regret it, Antonio," said Mario and his eyes were moist with emotion, "Come and see me next weekend before you go to London, and I'll show you all there is to know."

Antonio looked at him sharply, "You've arranged for me to go to London next week. You were *that* sure I would accept."

Mario smiled, "Yes, my boy. I rarely misjudge my people. They're expecting you in London next Monday. Now, let's get back to your party. That pretty little girl is waiting for you. If only I were a few years younger, you would have to watch your step, my boy."

"No chance, Grandpa," laughed Antonio, "She's mine."

Antonio thought about that as he went back to Beccy. She could be his. She would let him make love to her, but he was not sure if that was what he wanted. Beccy was not a girl with whom he could play around. She was too sensitive for a casual tumble in bed, He knew it would break her heart if he made love to her and then dumped her when he went off to London. He did not want to hurt her like that. There were plenty of girls who would sleep with him if he wanted sex, and there would be no hang-ups if he walked away afterwards. He sighed as he saw Beccy smiling at him. He would have to end it, and even that made him feel guilty.

Beccy cried when he told her later.

"I'm sorry, Antonio," she said, wiping the tears from her cheeks with her fingers, "I really like you, and I was hoping I could see you again."

Antonio held her tight and kissed her head.

"You will, Beccy," he said, "I'll be home some weekends. We'll go out then, and I'll phone you. Write if you like."

"No you won't," said Beccy miserably, "You'll forget me."

"Don't, Beccy," said Antonio softly when she started to cry, but he knew she could be right.

"How can I forget you? You're the prettiest girl in the City. Look, I want you to take this."

He took off his gold signet ring.

"Here, keep this, Beccy," he whispered, "keep it safe for me. The circle has no end. You always come back to where you started. I'll come, Beccy. I promise you."

He meant what he said, but it was not so much that Beccy had suddenly become important in his life, than the knowledge that his life would be here in Glasgow

What Price Ambition?

eventually. He could be a friend to Beccy when he was at home, a close friend, if that was what she wanted.
He kissed her passionately before he released her,
"Go on, it's late, I'll see you before I leave." he said, knowing that she was his whenever he wanted her, but revelling in the thrill and anticipation of stringing her along until he was ready.
Antonio walked back to the taxi which was waiting for him, and sank back into the seat as it took him home.
"Heavy night, Pal?" said the driver, for Glasgow taxi drivers are not known for their taciturn characteristics.
Antonio grinned, "Yes, a bit. I've just taken on the heaviest load a man could ever be asked to carry."
"So, when's the wedding?" said the driver,
misunderstanding Antonio's meaning.
Antonio laughed, but did not enlighten him, "Not for a while," he said, "I've got some living to do first."
"Good for you, Pal," said the driver, "You go for it."
"I intend to." said Antonio, and he smiled as the thought of his life ahead filled him with a huge sense of excitement and pleasure.

What Price Ambition?

Chapter 2.

New Beginnings.

The next few weeks in London were hectic for Antonio. He was taken to the bosom of the financial institution and set to work immediately to learn the business from start to finish. His Grandfather had booked him into a hotel
initially, but he wanted to find a flat for himself, and that occupied all his leisure time. Eventually, he found a place he liked in a large house in St. John's Wood. The elderly lady whose family had owned it for several generations, was finding it difficult to manage, and had turned the first floor into four flats. There was even a garage for his car, and his Grandmother arrived to help him furnish it.

"Now, Antonio." she said as they sat in the newly decorated room, "You have all that an ambitious young man needs. Don't throw it away. Have a good time, but always remember your responsibilities. Your Grandpa, Mario, sent this letter of introduction for you. Go and see Dimitri Ferolla. He will help you meet the right people, and Antonio, find yourself a nice girl."

"I've got a girl, Nonna. I'm quite fond of Beccy. She's my girl. That's not to say I won't go out with anyone here," he grinned, "But Beccy's the special girl in my life."

His Grandmother frowned, and she leaned forward.

"I didn't realise it had gone this far, Antonio," she said, "Beccy isn't the girl you should marry. You need someone strong."

Antonio laughed and patted her hand.

"I'm not planning to marry her, Nonna. I just like her. She's intelligent, well-educated, good fun and she's pretty." he grinned.

"But she's weak, Antonio." persisted Anna.

"Come off it, Nonna, you hardly know her. She's got firm views on most things."

Anna shook her head, "I'm sorry, Toni, but Beccy will let you down when you least expect it. I know. I've seen it many times. You should leave it to me. I'll find you a girl who is good enough to be your wife."

"Oh no you don't, Nonna. You just cool it, I mean it."

Antonio's eyes flashed with a purpose Anna recognised, and she nodded.

"Very well, I'll say no more, but you'll remember this conversation when it's too late."

What Price Ambition?

Antonio laughed, "Nonna, you're getting too heavy. This is a celebration. Let's chill out. I'll take you out to dinner." Anna smiled,, "I'd like that, Antonio , but I don't know about this chilling bit. I like my comforts."

Antonio laughed, "Just an expression, Nonna. I can see I'll need to educate you."

Antonio had no time to think in the following weeks, and before he knew it, autumn was changing the warm summer evenings to a coolier, more intense trip into the night.

Antonio was keen to learn at work, and with his persuasive charm, he was soon able to convince them that he could handle the work on his own. His confidence

in his own ability was substantiated when he did extremely well, and earned the personal praise of the Chairman who had employed him at his Grandfather's

request. The Chairman made a point of seeing him personally to offer his congratulations.

"Your Grandfather should be proud," he said, "It was a good move when we employed this young man, was it not, Evans?"

However, not everyone was pleased, and if he had known it, Antonio made an enemy that day. The pale blue eyes of the blonde haired man in front of him showed no emotion at all as he offered his hand to Antonio at the Chairman's

side.

What Price Ambition?

"Congratulations, old chap," he said, "You've done well for a new boy."

Antonio looked at him closely, "I'm sorry, I don't know your name."

The blue eyes flickered momentarily, "Of course you don't. I'm Ralph Beaton. You've just broken my record for the best newcomer. Well done."

Antonio's smile faded as he looked somberly at Ralph Beaton, for somehow, his felicitations did not ring true.

"I'm sorry. I wasn't trying to get one up on anyone. I was just doing the job to the best of my limited ability."

"Now, Beaton," said the Chairman, "All records are there to be broken. Mr. Agusta has had outstanding success, and I hope you're man enough to recognise it."

"Yes, Sir," said Ralph, "I didn't mean to belittle his efforts."

He said it with almost a sneer and Antonio knew that it was a lie, but he smiled.

"I'm sure you didn't, Beaton." he said quietly, deliberately using Ralph's surname to subtly, show his contempt for the other man.

The Chairman left in a flurry of scurrying executives, and Antonio went back to his work station. As he left, he heard Ralph Beaton speak to those around him who were still gathered there,

"He thinks he's the top cat," he said loudly, "We'll see how long he lasts without his influential friends."

What Price Ambition?

Antonio ignored him and got on with his work. He was going to a party the next night to meet the friend of his Grandfather for whom he had brought the letter.
Dimitri Ferolla's home in the heart of the Surrey countryside was more of a mansion than a house, set in a huge estate. Security was tight as Antonio drove up to the front of the house, and was searched before he went in. Ferolla himself was a large, average sort of middle-aged man, but he was impeccably dressed. The party he was giving was for his sister, Maria, whose birthday it was, and on whom he had spared no expense,
Antonio mingled with the guests after he had been introduced to Ferolla, and he danced with a couple of girls before he drifted to the bar and sat watching the revellers.
"Good party," said a voice at his side.
Antonio turned to look at the man sitting on the next stool.
"I suppose so." said Antonio with a shrug.
"You're not enjoying yourself, I take it," said the man and he smiled, "I'm Max Hunter."
Antonio studied the fine, handsome features and guessed that he would be about thirty five,
"Antonio Agusta he said and suddenly he laughed, "No, I'm not enjoying it, I came to see Mr. Ferolla, but I don't know why I bothered, I don't know what Grandpa thinks he can do for me."

What Price Ambition?

"Dimitri Ferolla is a very powerful man," said Max, and he glanced around as if he was nervous of something, "I told my friend, Steven, he shouldn't get involved, and It's probably good advice for you too. Ah, here's Steven now. Nice talking to you, Antonio. You take care now."

Max went off with his friend, and Antonio was so busy watching their departure that he did not notice the man who had moved to his side.

"Mr. Ferolla would like to see you." he said and took Antonio's arm.

Antonio looked at the man's hand on his sleeve, and the slowly turned towards him

"Get your hand off me," he said quietly. "I can walk on my own, fella."

The man's grip tightened, and Antonio saw the menacing glint in his eye for a second before he relaxed and smiled.

"Sure you can, son," he said, "For now. Come on, Mr. Ferolla doesn't like to be kept waiting."

Dimitri Ferolla was back at his table, and he waved his hand for Antonio to sit down next to him.

"Have a drink with me Antonio Agusta. I hope you found something to amuse you. I had a bit of business to take care of."

Dimitri looked towards his sister Maria who was sitting to one side and she raised her glass to him with a smile, but Dimitri did not enlighten Antonio.

What Price Ambition?

"You're better looking than your Grandfather, Don Mario." he said with a smile as he turned his attention back to Antonio,

Antonio laughed for his Grandfather was a big man with protruding eyebrows and an over-generous Roman nose.

"I think I take after Nonna. She was beautiful when she was young."

"So they say," said Ferolla, "My father knew her in the old Country. So, young Agusta, you're to inherit the Family business from Mario. It takes guts, determination and a belief in your birthright you must never forget. The world

is yours, Antonio, but you will also have responsibilities. The burden will sometimes be greater than you think a man can bear, but bear it you must. To you, Antonio Agusta. May those who have gone before protect you, and if you need any mortal help, contact me immediately. Here's my private number. What is it, Claudia?" he said impatiently as a girl approached him, "Can't you see I'm

busy."

Antonio glanced at the girl as she tossed her head, and bent her face towards Dimitri to whisper something to him. She had dark hair and smouldering eyes which seemed to be burning into Antonio's soul in that one brief glance.

What Price Ambition?

Dimitri listened for a second and then glanced at Antonio, and smiled slightly, "Not now, Sweetheart," he said and kissed her cheek, "We'll sort something out another time. Go and dance with the young man you invited."

When she left with another toss of her head, Dimitri shrugged and turned to Antonio with a smile, "My daughter, Claudia." he said, and changed the subject. They chatted for another half hour before he excused himself and Antonio left the party.

He drove back to the City, and went home. It was reasonably late anyway, and he intended to go straight to bed. However, as he passed the sitting room without putting the light on, he heard the answering machine bleep to tell him that there was a message. He crossed in the dark to the table and pressed the button.

"I'm sorry," said a voice, "I shouldn't have called,"

There was a pause, and something like a sob, "Antonio, I wish you were here." and she hung up.

Antonio frowned and played it again. It was Beccy. He looked at his watch, and the luminous hands told him it was past midnight. He had no idea why Beccy could be so upset, but he would probably wake her parents if he phoned now, so he decided to leave it till morning.

"May I speak to Beccy?" he said politely next morning as he sat finishing his coffee after breakfast. Absently, he watched the birds in the trees outside his window as he waited. The trees were losing their leaves now that autumn was drifting into winter.

"I'm sorry, Antonio," said Beccy's mother, "Beccy doesn't seem to be here. I don't know where she is I'm afraid."

Antonio thanked them, and put the phone down with a frown, Beccy had sounded upset last night and he was worried. He jumped when the phone rang, and he picked it up quickly hoping that it would be Beccy.

"Toni," said an unfamiliar female voice, "It's Virginia." Antonio frowned a second time and then he smiled. Virginia was one of the women who worked with him.

"Virginia," he said, "This is a surprise. What can I do for you?"

She laughed, "We're short of a man for squash, Darling," Come and join us, Toni. Be a darling."

"That's a bit energetic for a Sunday morning." laughed Antonio.

"Please, Darling we'll make it swimming if you prefer."

"Okay. Tell me where and I'll meet you at the pool. Give me an hour. I'm not dressed yet."

Virginia was older than Antonio. A single, unattached woman, and she made a great fuss of him when she arrived at the pool with another couple.

"Antonio," she called and kissed him on both cheeks, "Come and meet my friends."

What Price Ambition?

Virginia introduced him to the man and woman in their mid-twenties, and Antonio paused in surprise when the woman spoke Italian.
"Virginia, tells me you're Italian, and that your family is friendly with the Chairman at the bank." she said.
Antonio replied in Italian.
"Not quite. My Grandparents are Italian, and yes, they're friends of Mr. Marcos, Do you know him?"
The woman went on in Italian and Antonio noticed the quick intake of breath when she spoke."
"Oh I don't know him personally, but I know who he is. I did so want to meet someone in the Mafia, It must be very exciting."
Antonio looked at Virginia angrily.
"I'm not a circus act, Virginia. Sorry to spoil your little show, but I think I've got better things to do. Ciaou, babe."
He raised his hand and left the pool without looking back.
Next day, Virginia avoided him until they were alone for a few minutes.
"I'm sorry. I didn't mean to offend you."
"Well you succeeded," said Antonio shortly, "Just keep out of my face, Virginia.
I don't need you or your friends."
What Antonio said was not strictly true. He was lonely in London. He did not know anyone, and all he seemed to do at work was make enemies.

What Price Ambition?

Virginia shrugged and left him to his own devices, and Antonio went back to work.

He had only been seated at his desk for a few minutes when Ralph Beaton approached him.

"There's a phone call for you, old chap."

"Sorry, can't you take a message," said Antonio, "I'm in the middle of something."

"Those BAT investments in Hong Kong. I can do that for you."

Antonio looked up at him and saw a smile on his face.

"We have to work together, old chap. Go on, take your call."

"Thanks. I appreciate it."

He got up and left his desk to answer the internal phone. It was the Chairman's secretary.

"Mr. Marcos would like you to dine with him and his family on Friday."

Antonio did not hesitate. No-one refused the Chairman, especially one who was known as Don Philippo to his Family.

When he returned to his desk, Ralph nodded to the computer screen,

"All done,"

"Thanks." said Antonio and sat down.

He did not look at the screen for a few minutes as he prepared his next sheet, and when he did his heart lurched and skipped at least one beat. The transaction

What Price Ambition?

Ralph had handled for him showed a massive dive in profits. They would go ballistic.

Antonio threw his chair back and strode over to Ralph's desk.

"What the hell did you think you were doing, Beaton?" he said angrily.

"What is it, old chap?" said Ralph mildly, swinging his chair round to face Antonio.

"You know damned well what it is, you bastard. You deliberately set me up."

Antonio clenched his fists,

"I don't know what you're talking about, old chap." said Ralph, looking round him to the others who were watching them, "All I did was give you a message and answer your phone for you."

Antonio grabbed Ralph's tie, "You bastard!"

"Mr, Agusta!" said a voice behind him, "We don't want young men who behave like thugs in this office. Please close your station, and leave the office at once. I'll speak to you in the morning, Now, if you please! Everyone else back to work."

The section manager looked darkly at Antonio.

"You'll pay for this, Beaton." said Antonio as he left.

Ralph smiled, "I don't think so, Agusta. You made the loss. It's you who made the mistake."

Antonio did not stop to point out that he had not actually mentioned what was wrong, and the only place Ralph Beaton could have seen it was on his screen.

What Price Ambition?

Instead, Antonio left the office and drove like a man determined to have an accident to his flat where he threw his keys on the table next to the phone and pressed the message, button on his answering machine,
"Dimitri Ferolla here. Give me a call Antonio. As soon as you get in."
Antonio went to change his clothes into something casual first so that he had time to calm down, but his curiosity got the better of him and he went back to the phone.
"Hello, Mr. Ferolla," he said when he got through, forcing a cheerful note to his voice, "You wanted to speak to me."
Dimitri Ferolla laughed, "Well, it's more my daughter. She's done nothing but talk about you since she saw you at the party last Saturday. Her mother says we won't get any peace till we invite you over. Tonight at eight, Antonio. Nothing special, just a family dinner."
"I won't be very good company tonight, Mr. Ferolla"
"Oh, and why not, my boy?"
Antonio sighed and told Dimitri what had happened at work.
"Is that all, Antonio," laughed Dimitri, "BAT, you say. Just leave it to me."
Antonio stared at the phone after Dimitri had hung up. How on earth could he help? He wasn't into banking or even anything to do with the money market as far as Antonio knew. Dimitri Ferolla owned night clubs and

casinos with a chain of fast food shops under his control too.

Dinner that evening was very pleasant with Dimitri's daughter, Claudia, and Antonio enjoyed her bright, sparkling chat. Claudia was amusing, and she would not allow him to retreat into self-pity.

"Toni, you're so quiet," she complained with a laugh.

Antonio grinned at her, "It's just as well," he said cheekily, "You haven't stopped talking."

Dimitri laughed, "You tell her, Antonio. She never listens to me. Claudia, let the boy get a word in."

Claudia pouted her full lips at her father and scowled, but her eyes still sparkled with mischief and amusement.

Antonio smiled. Claudia Ferolla was a spoiled young woman, but she was just what he needed right now. She tossed her head and her black hair shimmered in the lamplight.

"So what is it you do for kicks, Toni?" she said, her eyes daring him to be controversial.

Antonio smiled, "I accept invitations to dinner with girls like you, Claudia. I think that's dangerous enough."

Dimitri roared with laughter, and Claudia pouted again.

"And then what?" she said with a catch to her breath, "What will you do tomorrow or the next day?"

Antonio looked boldly at her, "Take you out somewhere, a club maybe."

What Price Ambition?

"And what makes you think I want you to?" Claudia said haughtily.

"Mama mia" exclaimed Dimitri, "The girl's beyond me. Only three hours ago you were planning where he could take you."

"Dad!" said Claudia in embarrassment, "I did no such thing."

Antonio smiled, "So, where is it to be then?"

Claudia just shrugged and said nothing.

"Claudia Ferolla where are your manners?" said her mother, "Why don't you give them passes for your new disco, Dear?" I'm sure Antonio would enjoy it. Claudia isn't old enough to go to a club. She's just seventeen."

"I'm sorry, I didn't realise, Mrs. Ferolla, Ok, we'll go for the rave. I'll pick you up at eight tomorrow."

"I haven't said I'll go with you."

"Suit yourself. I won't ask you again."

Claudia got up from the table, "Excuse me Mum, Dad. I think I've got a headache coming on. Goodnight, Antonio."

Antonio stood up, "Eight o'clock. Don't keep me waiting." he called as she left the room hurriedly.

"Leave us, Mama," said Dimitri and smiled at his wife, "Come on, Antonio, let's have a brandy, I have some very nice Armagnac."

Dimitri put his hand on Antonio's shoulder as they walked to a small sitting room where he poured two brandies.

"She's young," he said, and he laughed, "You know how to handle her, Antonio. Just don't hurt her,. I want your word, Antonio."
Antonio nodded, "I'll treat her like sister, Mr. Ferolla.
"Well, I don't think Claudia will like that, but I don't want you sleeping with her. I know what young men are like."
"I understand. You don't have to worry. I'll take care of her. She'll be safe with me."
"Good," said Dimitri, and he patted Antonio's arm, "And don't worry about your little problem at work. I've taken care of it. Another brandy?"

Chapter 3.

Retribution.

Antonio stared at his portfolio in amazement as he brought up his current file on the computer. The large investment he had made which had made a thundering loss yesterday had recovered dramatically when they announced a
new deal with Goldfish Distribution Company at Subic Bay in the Philippines.
Subic Bay was a former United Nations base, now converted to a Freeport, and over which the Philippine customs authorities had no jurisdiction. Cargoes could come and go with impunity and the customs officials had no authority to check any of it.
BAT had been critiscised since 1993 for dealing with companies reputed to have Triad connections, which were exporting cigarettes illegally to China and Taiwan.
"Well done, Mr. Agusta," said the section manager, "That was an inspired move on your part yesterday."

What Price Ambition?

Antonio smiled and looked directly at Ralph Beaton.

"Yes, I had a good teacher," he said, "Isn't that right, Beaton?"

Later Ralph left his desk to go to the cloakroom, and Antonio followed him. Beaton was washing his hands when Antonio entered, and he looked up with a start when Antonio paused behind him.

"That was a bit of luck, Agusta," Beaton said.

Antonio moved closer so that Ralph could feel his breath on his ear,

"Luck had nothing to do with it," Antonio said quietly, "I have friends, Beaton. Powerful friends, and if you try anything like that again, you'll end up feeding the fish in the Thames."

Antonio jabbed him in the kidneys once, and Ralph Beaton doubled over in pain.

"That's a taste of what I can do if I really try," Antonio said, "You can thumb your nose all you like with your high and mighty friends, but in my world, power isn't measured on a piece of paper."

"You're a thug, Agusta," gasped Ralph, and Antonio hit him again on the other side.

"You're right, Beaton," he said, "Better a thug in a man's world than a wimp in yours, and you'd better remember it."

Antonio went back to his desk, and carried on with his work as if nothing had happened. He did not often use physical violence on anyone, but neither did he flinch

from it if he felt the situation needed it. He had needed to let Ralph Beaton know who was really top dog, and it gave him satisfaction to have made that point. However, even as he formed that thought he frowned. He was not
really into violence, and he had a fleeting feeling of shame. It passed in an instant, forced from his mind quickly when a new, exciting thought drove it out. He was seeing Claudia later and he did not want any dark thoughts in his mind when he took her out.

She was an attractive girl, and fiery, just the way he liked, but he would keep his promise to her father. She was taboo to him for anything other than good fun, and maybe a little light romance.

Antonio had not reckoned with Claudia. She met him in the hall exactly at eight as he had insisted.

"Wow! You look stunning," he said as she appeared down the stairs in a short, shimmering dress,

"Claudia, you might as well not bother to wear anything," said her father, "Do you want to be molested?"

"Dad, don't be silly, this is what everyone wears, and I'm sure I'll be quite safe with Toni."

"She'll be fine, Mr. Ferolla," said Antonio, "And we won't be late."

Claudia pouted at his words, but Antonio took her arm and led her to his car before she could say anything."

"Let's not go to the disco,"

What Price Ambition?

"Okay, where do you want to go?"
"Your flat. I want to go to bed with you."
Antonio looked startled at her direct approach.
"No way," he said, "I'm not planning to die yet."
"He won't know," said Claudia, knowing that Antonio was referring to her father,
"I'm not a virgin, you know." she added.
Antonio grinned, "So, I didn't know," he said, "But I'm still not risking it."
Claudia tossed her head and looked out of the window.
"So, what's it to be?" said Antonio, "The disco or a bar somewhere?"
"I don't care. You choose."
Antonio glanced at her as he drove. He would have liked to make love to her, but somehow he did not think she was as experienced as she wanted him to believe. If she was, she had retained that certain blush of innocence under the
skirts of womanhood.
He took her to a quiet bar he had found not far from his flat where he knew the bar staff well. They greeted him cheerfully when he ordered drinks.
"Nice one, mate," said the bartender, nodding in Claudia's direction, "Looks like you'll have your hands full tonight."
"With a bit of luck, Mark," laughed Antonio and. went back to Claudia.

What Price Ambition?

"What were you laughing at? That barman wants to mind who he's staring at."

"You shouldn't look so gorgeous. He fancies you."

"But you don't. Maybe I should go out with him."

"I didn't say that. Of course I fancy you. Here, I'll show you."

He put down his drink on the table and pushed her firmly against the back of the seat, cupping his hands over her breasts while he fiercely kissed her for several minutes.

She gasped when he let her go.

"You animal!" she panted, "What did you do that for?"

Antonio grinned, "It was what you wanted, wasn't it."

Claudia looked away, "No, not like that," she almost whispered, "I wanted you to love me, but I don't suppose you know anything about that."

Antonio picked up her hand and held it in both his.

"That wasn't the signal you were giving me. You propositioned me, remember."

"Yes, I'm sorry," she said and bowed her head, but only for a second.

Suddenly she tossed her black hair, and he saw the fire in her eyes.

"No, I'm not. I want to sleep with you, Antonio. Why won't you?"

"Because I promised your father, and I don't think you're as street wise as you make out. Have you really slept with other guys?"

What Price Ambition?

She bowed her head again.

"I didn't say I had. Technically, I'm not a virgin. I had to have an operation last year, but I've never had sex with anyone."

"Claudia, you're crazy. You don't know me. How do you know you'll like me? How do you know I'm not some sex-crazed maniac?"

She smiled, "My father checked you out. You're a nice boy from a nice family. You went to a nice school and you have nice friends. You don't have a regular girlfriend, but you were seeing a girl called Beccy before you moved to London."

"Jesus!" said Antonio, "I suppose you know what colour underwear I wear too."

"No, but I could take a look." replied Claudia quickly with a twinkle in her eyes.

"No way," said Antonio emphatically, holding up his hands, "Anyone with a father who goes to all that trouble is risky. I'm surprised he lets you go out with me."

"Antonio, you're changing the subject. Why won't you make love to me?"

"Like I said, I've got a few more years to live yet, Look, I *do* like you. Maybe when we've seen each other a few times I'll find the courage. I'm not into this feminist stuff anyway. I don't like to be pushed, Claudia, and

What Price Ambition?

you're just about running me off my feet. Take it easy, babe. We've both got a lifetime ahead of us."

"I suppose so," said Claudia, "I've never asked anyone before. I just couldn't help it when I saw you. I think it was love at first sight."

"Now I *know* you're crazy, girl," said Antonio, "Sex, love, you'll be hating me next."

"No, I won't," she retorted, "I like everything about you. Even that you won't sleep with me. I don't think you're afraid of my father. You're just a nice guy, Antonio."

Antonio smiled but he said nothing. What she thought of him was partly true.

He did not want to take advantage of her. He *did* like her, and he wanted to get to know her better, but he was also very much aware of the power that Dimitri Ferolla could wield. Antonio had a secure future ahead of him. A
prosperous and powerful career with the Family as long as he did his apprenticeship without slighting anyone's honour. Dimitri would make a bad enemy. He knew that, and he was prepared to do anything to avoid a conflict.

"I'm going to take you home," he said suddenly, "And I'll see you again at the weekend. You can come to my flat for lunch on Saturday."

Antonio saw her face light up with excitement.

What Price Ambition?

"Yes, my Grandparents will be there. They would like to meet you." he added with a smile for he knew it was not what she was anticipating.
Claudia's smile disappeared and her eyes flashed with annoyance.
"I don't know if I can make it."
"Yes, you can. I'll pick you up at eleven, and if it's alright
with your father, we'll go out somewhere in the evening."
She folded her arms and sat staring straight ahead in silence for the rest of the journey, and Antonio smiled as he glanced at her several times.
She knew who was boss now, and he would be nicer to her on their next date,
Claudia Ferolla was an exciting young woman, volatile and typically Latin. He liked her a lot, but he was not going to let her know that yet.
He was also planning to keep her parents happy, and it obviously pleased her mother when he took her home early. He knew he would have an ally in Mrs. Ferolla.
"My Grandparents are coining to town at the weekend," he said, "I've asked Claudia to come to lunch at my flat and meet them. I hope that's alright with you, Mrs. Ferolla." "Of course, Antonio," she said. Give them my regards. Goodnight." and she kissed him on the cheek.
He smiled as she shut the door, and he turned away. He

would marry Claudia Ferolla one day. As the thought came tumbling into his mind he stopped dead. Marriage was the last thing he had considered until now.

"You're the crazy one, Antonio," he said softly to himself, but even as he said it, he knew that his destiny was linked to Claudia's.

When he returned to his flat, there was another message on his answering machine. It was Beccy, this time coherent and purposeful. She had just telephoned to ask how he was, and could he call her if he got in before eleven.

He looked at his watch. Five minutes before the hour. He dialled Beccy's number.

"Oh hello, Antonio," said Beccy's mother, "I'm sorry, she's not here. She decided to go out. No, I don't know when you'll get her in. She's rarely here these days. To tell the truth, her father and I are worried about her. She seems so

moody since you went away. I don't suppose you could get back for a few days."

"Sorry, not this weekend, but I'll try and make it soon. I'll be home for Christmas if I can't. Tell Beccy to ring me when she's got a minute."

He tapped the phone thoughtfully. He and Beccy had not been that close. She surely was not pining for him. At least, he was that serious. He had looked upon her as a girlfriend he could call on when he went home to Glasgow.

What Price Ambition?

He would probably have slept with her eventually if he had still been there, but it was probably someone else who would have that pleasure now. Beccy wanted that sort of relationship.
Antonio went to bed and lay awake thinking about the two girls who had recently come into his life.
Beccy, fair, neat figure, quiet, studious and pretty. Claudia, dark, voluptuous, extrovert, completely spoiled and a fiery beauty. He liked them both, and he thought for a minute about stringing them both along at the same time. After all, they would never meet. He dismissed that idea quickly. He would treat them both as just friends and take his more intimate relationships somewhere else.
Antonio forgot about Beccy till after the weekend.
His Grandparents met Claudia, and she was the perfect young lady in their company.
"Antonio, this is the girl for you," said his Grandmother when he returned to the flat after an evening out with Claudia.
"Shouldn't you be in bed, Nonna?" replied Antonio avoiding the subject, "Do you know what time it is?"
"Don't fuss, Antonio," Anna said and waved her hand, "The old man needs his sleep. He's past it, but I don't tire so easily."
Antonio smiled, "Okay then, I'll get us a drink," and poured his Grandmother a brandy.
Anna did not give up.

What Price Ambition?

"You should marry, Claudia, Antonio. She's from a good family, and she's such a nice girl."

Antonio smiled. That was not how he would have described her passionate kisses in his car before he took her to her door.

Antonio sat down beside Anna and glanced at her.

"I will marry her one day, Nonna, but not yet, and I don't want to say anything to her. We've only just met. She's not the sweet young woman she would have you believe."

Anna laughed, "She's passionate, Antonio. Good Latin blood. She doesn't fool me with those dark eyes, but that's a good point. She's enough to hold your interest. You won't stray from that one. We'll have a word with her father."

She held up a slender finger as Antonio started to protest.

"Your bride must be suitably prepared. She will be marrying a future Don. Her parents must provide the proper dowry. No arguments, Antonio."

"Dowry!" exclaimed Antonio, "Girls don't have dowries these days."

"Girls belonging to the Family do," said Anna, "Especially if they're highly connected like Claudia."

"But I don't need money, Nonna. I'll be more than able to take care of a wife when the time is right."

Anna shook her head, "It isn't about money, Antonio, although that follows with the responsibility. Dimitri

What Price Ambition?

Ferolla will give you part of his Family holdings, and secure you a place on the Commission when you marry his daughter. He has a son so it won't be a majority holding, but it will be enough to let you expand our interests."

"This is crazy, Nonna. I'm sorry, I'm going to bed. Just you make sure that Claudia doesn't know anything about this."

"I think if I'm not mistaken, that young woman already has her eye on you, and she'll do just as her father tells her." said Anna with a smile.

Antonio hesitated with his hand on the doorknob. He was not sure that Claudia would do anything anyone told her. She was a fiery young woman, but he smiled and decided not to voice his thoughts. His Grandmother was a different generation.

"Goodnight, Nonna, sweet dreams."

Antonio was still thinking about Claudia when he went to work on Monday morning. If he had been more alert, he might have been aware of the conversation that Ralph Beaton was having with another of the dealers. As it was, Antonio did not look up till the man approached his desk.

"Hi, Alex, did you have a good weekend?"

"Great," replied Alex with a laugh, "Look, Toni, some of us are going ten pin bowling tomorrow night. Do you fancy it?"

What Price Ambition?

"Sure, thanks." said Antonio and wrote down the details.

Next evening, he joined Alex and the four other men and women, and enjoyed a pleasant night out with them. Afterwards, the others wanted to stay on for something to eat, but Antonio had promised to phone Claudia, and he left them with a wave to go to his car.

He ran lightly from the entrance across the dimly lit car park to the spot where he had parked his car, and put the key in the lock.

Suddenly, he was pushed hard against the car roof and he felt the pain sear through his face when someone behind him held him against the metal. He struggled violently to escape, but someone else took his other arm, and kicked

his legs apart so that he was off-balance.

"What do you want?" he managed to gasp.

"The Captain wants to teach you a little lesson in playing the game, mate. You shouldn't go threatening people. It's bad for your health."

He hit Antonio in the kidney region, and he almost blacked out with the pain.

Antonio struggled again, but he was kicked in the groin. This time his senses reeled into semi-consciousness, and he slid down the car. They hauled him up again, and Antonio swayed as one of them pulled him round before the blow the man delivered to his face sent him into oblivion.

What Price Ambition?

When he came round, he was lying face down on the ground beside his car. It was raining steadily and he shivered with cold. Even that slight vibration made him gasp with pain, and he moaned when he tried to pick himself up. With an effort he got to his knees, and opened the car door, his head pounding, and the excruciating pain bringing on waves of nausea. The steering wheel seemed
like a lifebuoy in the sea of his disorientated mind, and he clutched it desperately as he dragged himself into the driver's seat. He shut the door and sank back into the leather, holding his bruised and sore ribs. He could not
focus properly, and he closed his eyes in the semi-darkness for several minutes until he could think. When he opened them again, the glare of someone's headlights almost blinded him, and he held up his arm to shield his eyes. The movement wracked his body with pain, but he gritted his teeth and reached out with his other hand to turn the key in the ignition. Sweat ran down his forehead into his eyes, and he almost wept in frustration because his hand was so bruised and swollen that he could not turn it.
"Shit!" he exclaimed weakly, and tried to open the door to get out, intending to take a taxi. However, his body and mind at that moment did not seem to be connected, and he sank back in the seat. It took a few minutes to get his breath back and with an effort of pain-wracked concentration, he reached for the car

phone. His first attempt was abortive, and he did not quite reach it.

His body lurched forward and he collapsed against the dashboard, and lay there, his chest heaving for breath, till he felt able to make another concentrated effort. This time he made it, and picked up the receiver, but he could not

focus his mind to find a taxi number and squinted at it helplessly out of his puffy eyes.

"Claudia," he whispered suddenly, and his despair turned to hope. He could remember her number.

He dialled it and she answered herself almost at once.

"Antonio Agusta, you said you would ring me an hour ago." she stormed at him,

"Where have you been?"

Antonio gritted his teeth and breathed deeply.

"Cut the agro, Claudia, I need your help."

Beads of sweat were standing on his forehead, and Claudia could hear his laboured breathing.

"Antonio, are you alright?"

"No, can you drive, Claudia? Good. Get a taxi and come and get me. Never mind why, just do it!"

He told her where to find him, and then he drifted in and out of consciousness for the next hour till she arrived.

"Antonio!" she exclaimed in horror, for by that time his face was swollen almost beyond recognition.

What Price Ambition?

"Shut up, Claudia," he mumbled as she started to question him, "Just shut up, and help me out."

Claudia helped him to get into the passenger seat, and as he sat panting with the effort, she started the car and drove out of the car park,

"Turn left at the lights," Antonio directed, but Claudia ignored him and drove straight on.

"Claudia, did you hear. You should have taken a left back there."

"Now, you shut up, Antonio, I'm taking you home. You need a doctor. Mother will know what to do."

"Claudia, for Christ's sake, do as you're told for once."

He was trying to sound as if he was in charge, but his voice failed him miserably and the effort drained him.

He lay as still as possible for the rest of the journey, and did not say a word. He was past caring anyway. Even breathing hurt, and he did not have the strength to argue.

The body guards carried him into the house, and laid him down on the couch.

"Oh, my god!" exclaimed Mrs Ferolla, "No, take him upstairs to the guest room, Peter. I'll call the doctor."

The doctor was efficient and discrete.

"There's nothing broken, young man. You were lucky."

"Lucky!" whispered Antonio, and instantly regretted it, for even that effort hurt.

"Antonio, you poor boy. Don't say anything."

Mrs. Ferolla stroked his head.

What Price Ambition?

The doctor gave him an injection after he had treated his cuts and bruises, and Antonio drifted away from the pain. He tried to smile, but it was like a grimace.

"You should sleep, Antonio," said Claudia, "Here, I'll help you undress."

"No, you don't," he managed to blurt out, "Mrs. Ferolla get her out of here please."

Claudia was ordered from the room while her mother attended to Antonio, and soon he was asleep between the cool, fresh sheets in the Ferolla guest room.

When he woke up, Antonio saw the shadow of the figure by the window through half-closed eyes,

"Antonio, how are you, my boy?"

Dimitri turned from the window and approached the bed.

"What time is it? I have to be at work in the morning."

Dimitri laughed, "It's eleven thirty, and it is morning. Don't worry, I phoned your Boss, and told him you had an accident. Who was it, Antonio?"

Dimitri handed him some water, and sat down on a chair next to the bed as Antonio frowned.

He tried hard to remember.

"I don't know, I'd never seen them before. There were two,

big guys, lots of muscle, short hair. I reckon they were paid by someone, but who? I've never had any enemies."

What Price Ambition?

"It looks like you have now, my boy. What makes you think someone else was involved. They could just have been a couple of muggers."

Antonio shook his head and winced.

"No, they didn't take my wallet or the car. They wanted to hurt me, and one of them said something. Shit! I can't remember!"

"Take it easy. There's no hurry."

He gave Antonio some more water.

"The Captain, that's it. They called him Captain."

"Captain, like in the army or a football team?"

"I don't know." said Antonio and sank back on the pillow.

"Well, think about it Antonio, someone doesn't like you, and we'd better find them and ask them why. As Don, you can't afford to forgive and forget. It gives them the advantage."

"It's okay, Sr. Ferolla, I wasn't planning to turn the other cheek, but I don't suppose I'll see them again. There's no need."

"Yes, there is, Antonio," said Dimitri softly, "Someone has shit on my doorstep. At the very least he'll clean it up, and just maybe I'll rub his nose in it to teach him a lesson. When you remember, let me know. It's no longer just your

problem, Antonio. You must learn what honour means if you are to follow in Mario's footsteps,"

What Price Ambition?

The door opened and Claudia entered the room unceremoniously.

"Mum says what do you want to eat? You look terrible, Antonio."

"Thanks a bundle, I feel terrible. I'd like to soak in a bath if I could make it."

Before he could say any more, Claudia had whipped off the duvet.

"I'll help you up... oh, sorry." she said in embarrassment and turned away, for Antonio was naked in the bed.

"Claudia go and help your mother," said Dimitri, "And stay out of trouble. I'll call you when Antonio's ready. Tell your mother to make him something soft, pasta maybe, his lips are bruised."

"Yes, Dad," said Claudia and left the room in a hurry.

Antonio tried to smile, "She's quite a girl."

"Almost a woman," said Dimitri darkly, "She'll be the death of me. I'll have to find her a husband before she drives me mad."

Antonio's heart skipped a beat and he was about to say something but thought better of it, and accepted the robe Dimitri held out for him.

He was back in bed when Claudia brought him a tray.

"I'd like to stay, Dad," she said meekly and her father nodded.

"Don't tire him out. He took quite a beating."

"I'll take care of him. Here Toni, open wide,"

She lifted some food on the fork to his mouth,

What Price Ambition?

"I'm not helpless, Claudia," he said, but he relaxed against the pillow and accepted the food. It felt good to have her near him, and he was exhausted after his bath in any case.
"Who do you think did this? I would like to twist his scrawny neck till it breaks." she added fiercely.
"They would eat you alive, but thanks anyway. I've never had a woman fight for me."
Claudia looked at him with large black eyes as she continued to feed him.
"You didn't know *me* before. I'm not like your other women."
"You can say that again. What are you doing, Claudia? Stop that!"

She had placed the plate on the bedside table, and slid her hands down his chest to his stomach under the duvet.
"Claudia, I said stop it!" he repeated, and caught her hand,
"Don't you like it?"
Her eyes glinted like a child fulfilling a dare.
"Of course I like it, but it's neither the time nor the place.
Your father or mother could come in at any minute. Besides, I'm in too much pain."
"You're right,"

What Price Ambition?

She pulled the duvet up to his armpits, "When we make love it will be somewhere special."
"Claudia, you're doing it again. I don't want to make love to you. Will you get it through your silly head."
"Yes, you do," she said and tossed her hair.
Antonio sighed, for he knew she was right.
"More food woman, I'm still hungry,"
He laughed as he changed the subject.
She laughed lightly too, "The way to man's heart, I'm going to win your heart, Antonio. You just wait."
He could have told her that she already had his heart, but something made him bite back the words he wanted to say.
"I will with interest," he said, and then he suddenly sat up, knocking the plate out of her hand.
"Antonio! Look what you've done. What a mess."
"Sorry, I've just remembered something."
The mention of interest had jagged his memory. Ralph Beaton had a grudge against him.
"Look, don't worry about it," said Antonio as Claudia tried to wipe up the mess,
"Go and tell your father to check out Ralph Beaton, maybe he has a brother or father in the army. He works in my office."
Claudia went at once, recognising the urgency in his tone, and Antonio lay back and closed his eyes. Suddenly he was angry. He would deal with Ralph Beaton himself. He did not need Dimitri to fight his

battles. He had never run away from a fight in his life or shirked punishment if it was due.

Dimitri soon had the answer but Antonio was asleep again, and it had to wait till the morning

"Good morning, you're looking brighter this morning, but that black eye's a whopper."

Antonio touched his swollen eye and flinched,

"Yes, I owe someone for this. Did you find out about Beaton?"

"Beaton's a Captain in the TA. What's the hassle with him?"

"He's the guy who set me up when I first joined the company. You remember you helped me."

Dimitri nodded, "So he thinks he's clever."

"Mr. Ferolla," interrupted Antonio, "I want to deal with him myself."

Dimitri considered Antonio's words for a moment.

"You'll need some help," he said eventually, "When you've got a plan take Peter and Joe with you."

"Okay, thanks, I'll be in touch."

He stayed with the Ferollas for two more days, and then he went home to Glasgow for the rest of the week.

What Price Ambition?

Chapter 4.

Just Good Friends.

Antonio's Grandfather had spoken to Dimitri, and was waiting at the airport for him with the black Family limousine.
"What do you plan to do, Antonio?" Mario said.
"Nothing," replied Antonio with a slight smile as he leaned back into the plush leather seats, "I was hoping that Mum would spoil me for a few days."
"I didn't mean that. What are you going to do about this Beaton fella?"
Antonio sat up, "Teach him a lesson he won't forget, Grandpa." he said fiercely.
Mario smiled, "Good. Dimitri will help you. Accept his help, Antonio. I've arranged to see him to negotiate your marriage contract with his daughter."
"Grandpa!" said Antonio with start. "I'm not ready for that yet, and I haven't said anything to Claudia."
"There's no hurry for that Antonio, but the contract must be sealed. From what I hear the young woman won't take much persuading."

What Price Ambition?

"No, she wants me to sleep with her."

Mario looked at him sharply, "You must wait, Antonio. You must not take what isn't yours."

"I don't intend to, Grandpa. This one is different."

"By the way," said Mario changing the subject, "That girl next door has been round a couple of times asking when you're coming home, Maybe you could see her while you're here. Give her a little loving to keep her quiet, if you knew what I mean."

"You're a wicked old man," laughed Antonio, "Beccy isn't like that."

"They're all like that for the right man. This Beccy you can

afford to play around with while you wait for your bride."

"I don't think so, Grandpa," said Antonio with a frown, "I told you, Beccy isn't like that. She's more old fashioned than Claudia. She wants to wait for the man she's going to marry."

Mario turned his whole body in the corner of the car to look at Antonio.

"I think you're mistaken, Antonio. The girl has been seeing Nicholas Derwent. He's Alfred's son."

"Yes, I know him. He's a couple of years older than me. He's bad news, Grandpa. Why would Beccy go out with him?"

"Maybe he's the one to turn her head, but you know what I'm saying. We both know that Nicholas Derwent isn't the sort of man to spend money and time on a girl if she isn't giving him what he wants."

"I don't believe that Beccy would be fooled by him." Mario raised his hand, "Very well, Antonio. Just be warned." he said and dropped the subject.

However; the conversation came back to Antonio several times that evening and the next day, till finally, after lunch he told his mother that he was going to see his Grandmother. It was true enough, but he was also intending to see Beccy when she got home from work later.

He took a taxi because his mother refused to let him drive, and as it dropped him off at the entrance to his Grandmother's house, he saw a car pull out of Beccy's home and turn the other way. It was Nicholas Derwent whom Antonio recognised from his schooldays.

On impulse, he walked past Anna's house and down the drive to Beccy's door, his feet crunching noisily on the gravel.

The door opened almost as soon as he rang the bell, and Beccy stood there.

"Oh, I thought.,.. Antonio!" she cried and suddenly smiled, throwing her arms around his neck, "Antonio, it's wonderful to see you, but what have you been doing to yourself. That black eye. It must hurt something awful."

"Yes, it does a bit. Aren't you going to invite me in?"

What Price Ambition?

Beccy smiled and took his hand, "Of course, Mum is making some tea. Come and say hello."
He went with Beccy to the kitchen, and exchanged pleasantries with Beccy's mother, before she tactfully left them.
"How about a kiss?" said Antonio, "I've missed you, Beccy. I told you I would come back."
Beccy looked away, and did not move from the chair where she sat nervously turning the tea cup in the saucer.
"I'm seeing someone," she said, and looked at Antonio with what he thought was anguish in her eyes, "I'm sorry, Antonio."
Antonio sat down again, "That's okay. I'm pleased far you. I didn't expect you to wait for me. I've been seeing someone too." he added lightly.
"Is she pretty?" said Beccy in a whisper, and Antonio saw her fingers grip the cup.
"*I* think so. Grandpa tells me you're seeing Nicholas Derwent," he said casually, "I wouldn't have thought he was your type, Beccy."
Beccy looked away again.
"I know he's got a reputation, but he's nice to me. I like him."
"Why aren't you at work?" said Antonio, changing the subject.
"I don't work any more," said Beccy and this time she had a tremour in her voice, "I lost my job a couple of

months ago. I do some work for Nicholas. It pays well. Look, it's really nice seeing you, Antonio, but I've got to go and get ready. Nicholas is coming back for me in an hour."

"So, you won't come out with me. Beccy, he doesn't own you, and I see there's no ring on your finger, so how about dinner tomorrow?"

"No, I can't," said Beccy hastily, "And then she looked round anxiously as if she didn't want to be overheard, "Come round for lunch. Mum will be out tomorrow. We can have a chat."

"Okay, I'll see you tomorrow."

He bent to kiss her cheek, but she turned away abruptly with a nervous laugh.

"You really look funny with that eye." she said to cover her confusion.

"What's wrong, Beccy?" said Antonio, for he had caught a glimpse of something else in her eyes. Beccy was afraid of something or someone.

"Nothing's wrong. Why should anything be wrong?" she protested.

"Fine then I'll see you tomorrow."

He left Beccy and went to see his Grandmother. Anna was alone, and was horrified at Antonio's injuries.

"I'm alright, Nonna," he assured her as she fussed over him anxiously, "Have you seen Beccy since I've been away?"

What Price Ambition?

"So, you know," nodded Anna, "No, I haven't spoken to her for some weeks, not since she started seeing Nicholas Derwent. He doesn't seem her type at all."

Antonio chatted casually to Anna for a couple of hours, and then she insisted on sending him home in the limousine.

That evening, he went to see his friends, Drew and Rick to go over their plans for the car, but his mind kept going back to Beccy.

"Hey, Toni," laughed Drew, "Have you got brain damage as well. Concentrate, son. We need to get this, sorted out."

"Sorry, run it by me again, Drew."

Drew repeated what he had just said.

"So, what you're saying is that we need some investment in this to put together a full-time research team. That will take real money, guys."

"Well, the alternative is we call it a day," said Rick, "We've gone as far as we can as a hobby. I can't give it any more time. My business is just taking off,"

"Your business!" said Antonio in astonishment, for Rick had always been the easy-going one of the three of them. He had never had any ambitions to join the rat race.

"Rick grinned, "I've opened a chip shop. My Grandpa left me some money, and Dad persuaded me to invest it in something instead of blowing it on a trip round the world like I wanted."

What Price Ambition?

"Tough," laughed Antonio, "Still there's money in take-aways."
"There would be lots more if I didn't get all the hassle.".
"Hassle?" said Antonio, "What sort of hassle?"
"Oh, you know. Broken windows, gangs threatening the staff, thieving," said Rick with a shrug, "It goes with the territory."
"Do you know them?".
"Sure," said Rick, "You remember Callum Hill. Well it's him and his brother. I never did get on with them, and they're giving me grief now."
"He lives in the flats over by the green doesn't he?"
"That's the one."
"Leave it to me. They won't bother you any more."
Rick looked at Antonio curiously, but he nodded.
"Okay Thanks, Pal."
"You'll have to make a donation, of course," said Antonio, and Rick nodded again.
"No problem, Toni. Just send round the collection box."
The two young men fenced words in innuendo, each knowing what the truth meant, but not wishing to voice it openly.
"Well, let's hope you can fix our dilemma so easily," laughed Drew, "I can't afford to finance the car any more. I'm getting married next year."
Antonio punched him,
"I thought you had greater ambitions than that. What's wrong, you losing your touch, Pal?"

What Price Ambition?

"He's in love," laughed Rick, "Or maybe it's got something to do with the fact that her daddy owns a couple of garages."

"Shut up," said Drew, "We're in love. I'm getting married because I want to."

"I'm not knocking it," said Antonio, "I plan to join that club one day too."

"Oh! Who is she then?" Not Beccy!"

"No, not Beccy. You don't know her. She lives down south."

"Beccy's screwing up her life anyway, Pal," said Rick, "She's with that dick, Derwent."

"Yes, I know."

"You know he's into drugs, Toni?" said Drew, "Word is he's running pushers throughout the west of the City and down the coast too."

"Christ. No, I didn't know. I'll speak to Beccy. I'm seeing her tomorrow."

Rick and Drew looked at one another.

"Watch it, Toni," said Drew, "He's bad news and he won't like it if you're seeing his girl."

"Tough. Anyway, I'm not dating her, just having lunch with an old friend... So, what are we going to do about this car. Are you still planning to race, Drew?"

"Sure, my future father-in-law is keen on motor racing. He's offered to sponsor me."

"Why don't you go for the big time, Drew? Go for a test with one of the major formula one teams."

What Price Ambition?

"Do you think I'm ready for that?"

"Of course you are. You've got a good track record. You're the right age and you have no ties yet. Let's put the RAD modification on hold for a couple of years. By that time the patent will be through, and we can develop it then."

"OK, I'll buy that," said Rick, "In two years we'll all be in a better position to finance it."

"Great," said Drew, "Let's go to the pub and celebrate. God knows how I'm going to explain this to Susie."

"Tell her it's for your future together," said Rick, "or better still, that you want to be able to give her the most romantic honeymoon ever. She'll go for that."

"Just tell her you're doing it," said Antonio, Don't let her rule you, Pal. They like a man to be a man anyway."

Rick and Drew put their arms round Antonio's shoulders.

"Tell us more, Toni," said Drew, "Who *is* this woman who likes a masterful man?"

They went off into the City where they had grown up together for a night out as they had done many times before.

Antonio was more eager than he cared to admit about seeing Beccy next day, and he arrived a few minutes early in his mother's car. He frowned when he saw the other car parked at the front of the house, for it belonged to Nicholas Derwent.

What Price Ambition?

He hesitated for only a moment, and then he got out of his car and rang the doorbell. It opened almost at once, and Antonio was face to face with Derwent.

He had his jacket slung over his arm and his tie was loose around his neck.

"You're early. She wasn't expecting you for another half hour. You'd better watch it or I might get jealous." he smiled.

It disturbed Antonio that Beccy had told Derwent he was coming, but he just looked at him stonily, "Where's Beccy"

Derwent laughed, "She's getting dressed. She's a hell of a lay, mate."

Antonio's heart leaped as if a knife had been stuck in him.

"You low life," he hissed at the man who stood arrogantly in front of him, "Beccy deserves better than you."

"You, you mean," sneered Derwent, "But you left her, Agusta. I found her crying in a night club, drunk and being mauled by two louts who had picked her up. She needed a friend. I helped her and she was grateful. She gets more grateful by the day. She's one accommodating young woman. Look, screw her if you want to. I'm getting tired of her anyway."

"You bastard!" said Antonio, and he hit Derwent in the gut, hard and straight with all the hatred he could muster.

What Price Ambition?

Derwent doubled over, and backed out of Antonio's reach to make painfully for his car.

"That was a mistake, Agusta," he called to Antonio as he got inside, "You'll pay for that, the Don's Grandson or not."

Antonio watched him go, and then he went into the house and shut the door.

"Beccy," he called, and he heard her scramble hastily in her room before she came downstairs.

"Antonio, I wasn't expecting you yet. Nicholas has just left. Did you two meet?"

"We met. Beccy, you don't need him. What possessed you to get involved with him? He doesn't love you."

Beccy walked past him into the kitchen.

"I need him," she said quietly and turned to look at Antonio over her shoulder, "He looks after me."

Antonio stared for a minute, and then he saw it in her eyes.

"No, Beccy!" he said sadly, "You're using drugs."

He grabbed her arm, "Beccy this is crazy. You'll kill yourself. How could you let him treat you like this... like a whore."

Antonio guessed that Beccy was probably trading sex for the drugs to which she had become addicted.

"I told you, Nick looks after me. He gives me more money than I could ever earn in an office."

What Price Ambition?

"At what price, Beccy? He doesn't even respect you. He just offered you to me like some second hand car he was trading in, Beccy, what happened to your dreams?"

"You went away," whispered Beccy, "I had no-one. I went to the clubs, danced, drank, met people, but it wasn't like it was with you. I loved you, Antonio."

"Beccy, don't. I never promised you anything. We were friends, that's all. You'll find the right man one day."

"I have found the right man. I like Nick and I need him."

"You've got to stop using."

"Go away, Antonio," said Beccy angrily, "Stay out of my life. You've no right. You can talk anyway. It's your family behind it."

Antonio grabbed her shoulders, and made her look at him.

"What are you talking about? Behind what?"

Beccy laughed harshly, "The drugs of course. What do you think? I take the packages for Nick to the ice cream vans, your Grandfather, Mario's vans. They sell the drugs to the punters from the vans on the streets."

"You're lying. Grandpa would never sanction that, and what has Derwent to do with him?"

"Get real, Antonio. Nick works for your Grandfather. He runs the pushers and collects the money. Your Grandpa isn't the kind old man he would have you believe. Have you ever tried it, Antonio? Here, I've got some smack.

What Price Ambition?

It's good stuff. None of your rubbish. We could shoot it up together. Come on, let's go upstairs. It's good when you make love as well."
Antonio shook off her arm, "Beccy, stop this, please. You can't destroy your life for this guy."
"Not for Nick," said Beccy softly, "For you, Antonio."
Antonio shook his head slowly, and backed away from her.
"No, Beccy, you're not laying this on me. You're responsible for your actions. You said yes when you should have told him to get lost. If you have any feelings for me, you'll flush that stuff down the pan, and let me take you to a doctor. Come with me now, Beccy."
He held out his hand to her, and she slowly moved towards him, her eyes big and frightened,
"I'll come with you, Antonio," she said, "But I want you to promise me that you will help me. I want you to promise that you won't leave me alone again."
"I won't leave you alone."
Beccy almost threw herself into his arms.
"That's all I ever wanted, Antonio. Hold me and make it all go away."
Antonio held her and stroked her hair gently, dismissing the guilt he felt, for he had carefully worded his reply not to commit himself to something he could not give Beccy.

What Price Ambition?

"Come on, let's get you some help," he said, and Beccy allowed him to take her next door to his Grandmother.
Anna rang a clinic where they treated drug problems, and she went with Antonio to take Beccy there.
"Don't worry, Antonio she'll be fine. You go home and I'll speak to her parents. Grandpa will see to the bill."
Antonio frowned. He wanted to ask Anna about the ice cream vans, but he could not bring himself to utter the words. If his Grandfather knew about it all along, he was not sure what he should do, and if Mario did not know, someone else in the organisation did. It weighed heavily on Antonio, for whatever he decided to do would ultimately reflect on him, and he was not sure of his
ground. He had to tread carefully, so he decided not to do anything for the time being.
He went to see Beccy for the next two days, and she was trying hard to cope with the programme she had been set to free herself of her addiction.
"I can do it if I know you're here," she said as she sat gripping Antonio's hand.
"Beccy, that's what I wanted to talk to you about," said Antonio, knowing that what he was going to say would not go down well, "I'll always be here for you to talk to, but I've got to go back to London tomorrow. I've got to go to work."
Beccy stared at him with her eyes full of horror and fear.

What Price Ambition?

"You can't leave me. I can't do it without you. You mustn't leave me, Antonio. You promised."

Antonio sighed, "I said I would always be here for you, Beccy, and that still stands. I can phone you, and you can have my mobile. You can phone me whenever you want."

He reached in his jacket to get the phone, but Beccy knocked it to the floor and stood up. She did not cry or raise her voice. She stood in front of him like a woman turned to stone, rigid with fear, and the single purpose she had in her mind.

"Antonio, I'll kill myself if you leave me now. I mean it."

She backed away from him as he got up and tried to take her in his arms.

"Beccy that's silly," said Antonio, not knowing how to handle this sudden crisis.

"I'm not worth it. I love you." said Beccy, and this time a tear rolled down her cheek, "I don't want you to go. I can't live without you. I *won't* live without you."

Antonio turned away from her for a moment and closed his eyes in frustration and some desperation. When he turned towards her again, his eyes were dull and devoid of expression.

"Alright, if the doctor says it's okay, you can come with me for a couple of months till you get yourself together. I have to go to work tomorrow but you can come with me to London."

What Price Ambition?

Beccy laughed and cried at the same time, and she threw her arms around his neck.
"Oh, Antonio, I promise you won't regret it." she sobbed, "I'm so happy, Antonio."
Antonio rested his chin on her head, and he felt a dread take hold of his heart. He could not be responsible for Beccy harming herself, and he did not know what else to do, but he was not happy with it. All he could hope for was that she would see reason in a few weeks. He would get her to attend another clinic in London, and she would realise that she was wrong.
The doctor took pains to tell him what a big responsibility he was taking on, and his mother was furious, His Grandmother was even less sympathetic, probably for the first time in his life.
"Nonna, I just can't leave her. It's my fault she's like this."
"You know very well that isn't true, Antonio. She's manipulating you, and you've fallen for it. That girl is trouble. I told you right from the start. Don't be fooled by the pathetic, little girl act she puts on. She's decided that you're a better catch than Nicbolas Derwent, She wants the Don, not one of the lieutenants."
Antonio heard the Family reference Anna had just made.
"You knew he's working for Grandpa."

What Price Ambition?

"Yes, of course I do. He manages the fleet of ice cream vans, and he does, very well too, but he's an arrogant young man. I've told Mario to watch him."
"Nonna he gave Beccy the drugs. Does Grandpa know anything about a drug racket?"
Anna did not give him a direct answer.
"You know I don't get involved in business. Maybe Mario hasn't got a tight enough rein on that boy. Now, don't you be using anything, do you hear." she added sternly neatly changing the subject.
Antonio smiled, "I don't need drugs, Nonna. I find life stimulant enough to give me a high."
"And how's that invention of yours coming along?" said Anna with some relief that she had been given an opportunity to talk about something else, "Is it still your ambition to get it manufactured?"
"Oh yes, more than ever. Drew is going to try out for Formula One. He's good enough, but I'm not sure who you are doesn't count for more than how good you are in these circles."
"Tell Drew to come and see your Grandpa before he goes. We'll see what we can do. Now, if you're determined to tie yourself to that silly girl, you make sure it's not legally. Remember, you've been promised to Claudia Ferolla,"
"Oh shit! Sorry Nonna. I didn't think about it, did I?" How can I see Claudia with Beccy in tow? She'll never understand that there's nothing in it."

What Price Ambition?

"No, I don't suppose she will, especially when Beccy is expecting more than friendship."
"Well, that's all she's going to get. A few months ago I might have slept with Beccy. She was a nice girl, but not now. I don't fancy her any more."
Anna sighed, "Antonio you've taken on a heavy load, and if you're not careful, your knees will buckle under the weight. Leave Beccy here. Let the hospital handle her."
Antonio shook his head, "I can't Nonna. I owe her that much. She thought I loved her, and maybe I did give her that impression. Anyway, I have to put it right. I'll give her a couple of months. Don't worry; I have no intention of getting involved with her."
Anna hugged him, "Antonio, you have a lot to learn about women. Get rid of her soon, or you'll live to regret it. You should listen to your old Grandmother."
"Antonio's father too had something to say about it and when he took Antonio to pick up Beccy before they went to the airport he got the opportunity.
"Your mother is very disappointed, Antonio. We know that your Grandpa is negotiating with the Ferollas for you. Living with this girl could jeapordise that arrangement. I thought you were keen on Claudia Ferolla."
"I am, Dad, and that hasn't changed. I'm taking Beccy with me to help her recover. I won't be living with her like that."

What Price Ambition?

His father looked at him in disbelief.
"I'm not going to sleep with her," Antonio repeated quietly, "She can have the guest room."
His father shook his head.
"Your crazy, son. You don't live with a girl like that and expect to be just pals with her."
'A girl like what, Dad?"
"You know," said Giorgio in embarrassment, "Come on, Antonio, it's common knowledge she was knocking around."
"She thought she had a future with Derwent, but he was just using her. He was the only one, Dad. Beccy was a nice kid till she met that scum."
"I'm sorry, Antonio. I shouldn't listen to your mother's gossip. I thought... never mind. It's still a funny situation for you to put yourself in, and the Ferolla girl might not see it the way you do."
"I can handle Claudia," said Antonio with more conviction that he felt, "And as soon as Beccy is well, I'll bring her back, I have to do this, Dad. It's because of me that she's in this mess."
"Okay, son, I understand. Just remember to reach out and ask for help if you get out of your depth."
Antonio hugged his father.
"You know, Dad, I sometimes wish I could be like you, but it's here, driving me, and I don't seem to have any control over where I'm going."
Antonio thumped his chest.

What Price Ambition?

"You have your Grandfather's spirit," said Giorgio, and squeezed the hand he held,
"Let's go get Beccy."
Giorgio wished his son well at the airport in the Italian they had both learned at their mother's knee.
"Ciao, Antonio," he said softly and hugged him.
Giorgio had always loved the language, and the Country where his parents were born. He was a gentle man who had a passion for painting, and he did not want the responsibility which went with the family. He had given up his place at Mario's side in favour of his own son who had the inclination for it. There was no shame to it, rather honour that that he had recognised his failings so that Antonio could be schooled to take over. Antonio was the person for the job, and he would slip easily into the way of it just as Mario had done.

Chapter 5.

The Contract.

For the next few weeks Antonio worked hard during the day, and when he collected Beccy from the clinic on his way home, he took her back to the flat and watched television or played music. They talked too, and Antonio was content to let the world run by him for a while.

He changed his mind about telling Claudia about Beccy, and he deliberately kept away from her. However, one evening, as he and Beccy were just finishing dinner, the phone rang.

"Mr. Ferolla," said Antonio in surprise when he answered it, "Sure, I'm not doing anything this evening. I'll see you in an hour."

Dimitri Ferolla had practically summoned him to his house, and although Antonio tried to sound pleasantly casual, his heart was pounding inside his chest. He sensed that Dimitri was not pleased about something, and he did not want to be on the receiving end of his anger.

What Price Ambition?

Beccy was not keen for him to leave her, and there was no reasoning with her in the strung up state she was still in, so all he could do was make her take a sleeping pill, promising that he would be no more than three hours.
He slammed his car door and ran to the entrance to the Ferolla house. The door opened even before he rang the bell, and the security guard took him to the small sitting room where Dimitri stood by the fire. Claudia was curled up on a couch on one side of him, and her mother on the other with a glass of wine in her hand,
"Antonio," said Mrs. Ferolla, "How nice to see you. Come and sit beside me. Are you feeling better now?"
"Yes thank you, Mrs. Ferolla," replied Antonio politely, but he hesitated as he looked at her husband for permission to sit down.
Dimitri waved his hand, and turned to Claudia.
"Claudia, get Antonio a drink."
"Thanks, just coke, I'm driving."
Claudia got up silently and poured the fizzy liquid into a glass and handed it to Antonio, still without a word.
"You look wonderful. I've missed you."
Claudia tossed her head and returned to the couch where she sat silently twisting her hair in her fingers and glared at Antonio.
He looked at Dimitri and then at Claudia.
"Have I done something to offend you?"
"Claudia seems to think you've got someone else," said Dimitri, "I won't beat about the bush, Antonio. It's one

thing to have a bit on the side, but quite another to openly flaunt your lovers."

"I'm sorry, I don't understand," said Antonio, for the moment completely forgetting about Beccy.

"A woman answered your phone yesterday when I phoned, and again today. Who is she?"

Antonio got up and crossed to the other couch to sit beside Claudia.

"Claudia, you've got it all wrong, I swear to you, Mr. Ferolla, there is no other woman in my life, Beccy is a friend. She's staying with me for a while till she's better."

Dimitri stared at Antonio for a second and then he nodded.

"Very well, Antonio. Do you hear that, Claudia? Now let's have no more of this nonsense. Jealousy doesn't suit you."

"But Dad, I don't want him to have her in his flat. It makes me look very silly."

This time Antonio replied directly to her.

"You *are* silly, Claudia," he said firmly, "You should have asked me instead of running to your father with your tales. Either you love me or you don't, and if you do, you'll trust me. I would like to know if you trust me, Claudia, for if we don't have that, we can never have a marriage."

"Dad, make him stop. He can't talk to me like that."

Dimitri smiled and looked at his daughter.

What Price Ambition?

"Yes, he can, mia bellissima. He's the man you want, isn't he? Antonio is right. It's not your business."
"Look why don't you come over and meet Beccy tomorrow," said Antonio trying to defuse the situation, "She isn't ready to go out anywhere, but I cook a mean pasta when I put my mind to it."
"Antonio, you should never volunteer for anything in the kitchen," said Dimitri, "That's women's work."
"Dad, that's so old fashioned. Antonio and I will have a partnership when we marry, not a master and slave relationship."
Dimitri laughed, "So, you're a new man, Antonio. I was hoping you would keep her busy having my grandchildren. We want dozens of bambinos."
"I'll do my best, Mr. Ferolla," laughed Antonio, "But it's a long way off. We're not even engaged yet."
"You haven't asked me to marry you, Antonio Agusta," said Claudia, and her eyes flashed haughtily at him, "I might say no."
"And pigs might fly," laughed Antonio.
Claudia got up and stamped her foot in a tantrum. "You're so conceited. I don't know what I ever saw in you. You can call off the contract, Dad. I wouldn't marry *him* if he was the last man on earth."
"You see what you're getting Antonio," said Dimitri and raised his hands in a gesture of helplessness, "Are you sure *you* want *her*?"

What Price Ambition?

Antonio grinned, "Oh yes, I'm sure," he said, and his heart beat faster at the thought of Claudia in his arms. "Claudia is like her father." said Mrs. Ferolla who had been watching the comedy with some detachment, "She throws tantrums to get attention, and then butter wouldn't melt in her mouth when she gets her own way."

"Mother! I meant it. Antonio." she turned furiously to him, "I *will not* be taken for granted. If you can't make an effort to create a little romance for me, then I won't marry you. Do you hear, Dad?"

She turned and rushed out of the room, banging the door to the echoes of her father's demands to return.

"She'll calm down," Dimitri said apologetically. "But maybe you should make a little effort, Antonio, just to keep her happy. A Family contract is one thing, but two people getting married is something which needs a little romance, isn't that so, Mama?"

Antonio noticed the wistful smile as Mrs. Ferolla nodded. A look which told him that much of the romance had gone from her life, and he felt guilty that he had started off on the wrong foot with Claudia. He did not feel romantic with Claudia. He felt excited, and bursting with love for her, but he had never felt the urge to sing her a song or write her long love letters. He thought briefly of the girls in his past. There had been a couple he wanted to impress with something special and wined and dined them, sent them flowers and bought them gifts. He should do it for Claudia.

"Leave it to me, Mr. Ferolla," he said suddenly, "She won't know whether she's on her head or her heels when I've finished, Goodnight, Mrs. Ferolla. I'll pick Claudia up at seven tomorrow."

"No, don't do that, Antonio," Mrs. Ferolla said, "It's such a long way for you to drive. I'll send her in the car and Joseph can bring her home again, I hope your friend gets well soon."

Antonio knew that she was saying gently to him that he should get rid of Beccy if he wanted his life with Claudia to run smoothly. Mrs. Ferolla had a knack of stating exactly what she expected wrapped up in the less obvious niceties of polite conversation.

He was thoughtful as he drove back to the flat. Maybe he had been too impulsive to bring Beccy with him, but she was doing so well at the clinic. He could not tell her she could not stay with him any longer. Beccy needed him and he felt that he could not abandon her a second time.

He let himself into the darkened flat. All was quiet and he was careful not to make any noise which might wake Beccy. She had obviously taken his advice and gone to bed. He went straight to his room and undressed in the dark before crossing to the bed.

He pulled back the duvet and braced himself for the coolness of the sheets on his skin. However, the bed was warm, and as he pulled the duvet round him, he suddenly stiffened. He put out his arm, and the figure beside him stirred.

"Antonio," Beccy murmured, and turned over to wrap her arms round his chest, "I thought you would never come home."

Antonio felt his body tingle at her closeness, and he shivered as her fingers moved down his chest.

"Beccy, what is this?" he said quickly and sat up abruptly, switching on the light.

"Antonio, let me hold you," whispered Beccy and she kissed his lower torso.

He roughly pushed her head away from him.

"Stop this, Beccy. I don't want to sleep with you."

Beccy looked up at him, tears in her eyes.

"Please don't say that, Antonio. I need you to love me. Please make love to me."

Antonio got out of bed, suddenly feeling vulnerable in his nakedness. He grabbed his robe.

"Beccy I never intended this. I can't. I'm engaged to someone, a girl."

Beccy laughed hysterically.

"I didn't think it would be a boy," she said, and the laughter dried up suddenly, like someone cutting the phone line, "You can't mean that, Antonio. I love you. We're going to be good together. We'll get married if that's what you want. I'll be a perfect wife, you'll see. Please come to bed, Antonio. I'll show you."

What Price Ambition?

"Didn't you hear what I said? I have a girlfriend. I'm not interested. You're my friend, Beccy. I'm helping you get well because you're my friend, nothing more."
Beccy sat up and pulled the duvet round her chin, and stared at him with huge, drug-damaged eyes.
"I'll kill myself, Antonio. I need you. I won't let you marry anyone else. You can't. I know you love me."
Antonio looked at her and knew she meant it. He crossed to the bed and sat on the edge, holding both of Beccy's hands in his.
"Beccy, this is silly. You know I'll always be here for you. We'll always be friends, even when I marry Claudia, but we can never be lovers. I don't love you, Beccy." he said desperately.
"You're lying," she cried, "You told me you would come back for me. You gave me your ring. See, I've never taken it off."
She jerked her hand from his and grasped the ring she wore an a chain round her neck.
"Oh, Beccy, Beccy, I'm sorry. I didn't intend that to be any more than a token of our friendship. Of course I'll go back to Glasgow, and I'll see you there, but as a friend, Beccy. I don't love you, and I'm sorry if you got that impression."
Beccy shook her head in disbelief.
"No," she whispered, "I've thought of nothing else, Antonio. All the time I was with Nicholas I pretended he was you."

What Price Ambition?

Suddenly, she threw back the duvet and jumped out of bed. She had a good figure, and the sight of her naked body rippling as she almost ran out of the room, made him ache with a need he found hard to ignore. With a sigh, he shut the door and climbed into bed. He would speak to Beccy in the morning, for he did not trust himself to go to her now.

He was just about to put out the light when the door was thrown open again, and Beccy stood there. She was wearing a cotton nightdress and the teddy bear printed on the front somehow seemed to leer as it heaved against her breasts.

Beccy held up her fist.

"I've taken two. I'll take all of them if you don't sleep with me."

Antonio sat bolt upright for a second time, fear gripping him.

"Two what?" he said, dreading her answer.

"Jellies." Beccy replied.

"Where did you get them?" said Antonio and got out of bed, pulling on his robe again.

"I brought them with me just in case," she said, and held the handful of pills to her mouth.

"I don't want to live without you, Antonio. Please say you love me. It's all that's kept me going. I haven't touched anything since you came back for me, I swear I haven't."

What Price Ambition?

She sank to her knees in front of Antonio and the pills roiled across the floor to his feet like the chocolate smarties he used to play with as a child.
He bent down and lifted her to her feet, and held her in his arms.
"It's okay, Beccy," he said softly and kissed her hair, "You'll be fine. I promise. I won't leave you,. Let's go to bed."
He made love to her gently, and she cried into his shoulder.
"I love you, Antonio. Please say you love me."
He kissed her but he did not reply and he closed his eyes tightly against the image of Claudia which filled his mind. He could not find the words to lie to her, but he did not love her. He did care for her, and she needed him. He could not see a way out of this mess. He wanted to marry Claudia Ferolla. He was sure he loved her. She certainly excited him. Beccy felt good in his arms. She was soft, feminine, and loved him passionately with her body and her heart.
Despite himself, he had enjoyed making love to her, but even in the arms of passion, he did not love her. How could he tell her that? It would destroy her, and he did not want her death on his conscience.
Antonio lay awake most of the night, tossing thoughts and ideas around in his head. How could he handle this? Claudia was coming to the flat the next evening to meet Beccy, but he could not allow that to happen now.

What Price Ambition?

Beccy would make demands on him which would alienate Claudia and he would lose her.
Beccy, Claudia. Claudia, Beccy. He had no option. He had already made his choice, Beccy needed him, and he would have to stay with her until she was strong enough to go it alone. He hoped Claudia would understand, and want him,
but he knew that it was an improbable thought.
He had not resolved his dilemma when he picked Beccy up after work. She did not even want Claudia to come to the flat, and when Antonio mentioned it on the drive to the flat, she threw a tantrum.
"Phone her and tell her not to come," she sulked in the car on the way home, "I want to cook you a nice dinner and then we can make love."
Antonio glanced at her
"Beccy, I can't put her off, and I want you to promise me that you won't tell her that we're sleeping together. As far as Claudia is concerned, we're friends.
Beccy, please promise me."
"No, I don't want to see her," said Beccy sullenly, "I don't want you to see her either."
Antonio braked hard and the car shuddered to a stop with the screeching of tyres behind him as the other drivers were forced to take evasive action to avoid him. Antonio was oblivious to the chaos he was causing on the busy road, and he turned to Beccy and gripped her arm.

What Price Ambition?

"You're hurting me, Antonio. Let go my arm."
Antonio released her. He knew he was playing dangerous games with everyone's emotions, but he had to get a commitment from Beccy.
"Don't ever dictate to me, Beccy," he said softly and evenly, "You've got your way this time. I'm not going to send you away, but don't push me or I'll send you home and you'll never see me again. Do you understand?"
He didn't wait for her answer before he put the car in gear again and drove on in silence.
Beccy said no more and went straight to her own bedroom when they reached the flat.
Antonio threw his jacket on the couch and poured himself a drink which he downed quickly, and then he flopped down and closed his eyes. He could not let Beccy rule his life. She did not want him to have any life. He was so wrapped up in his problems that he jumped when Beccy spoke to him.
"I'm sorry, Antonio. Please don't be angry. I love you, and I don't want to share you with anyone."
She sat down beside him and kissed his ear.
"You'll love me, you'll see. You like me a little, don't you?" she whispered,
"Yes, I like you, Beccy," Antonio said   wearily, "But you're wrong, I'll never love you the way you want. You should find yourself a man who will."
"I want you. Please don't see *her* tonight."

What Price Ambition?

Antonio sat up and pushed Beccy away.

"I'll see anyone I like, Beccy," he said angrily, "It was a mistake to invite Claudia here. When she arrives, I'll take her out for dinner, and there's no point crying. I've made up my mind. Give me those pills you had. I said give them to me, Beccy."

His voice was icy, and Beccy moved away from him.

"Get them now!" he ordered, and she ran to her room to get them for him, fearful of the look in his eyes.

Antonio put the drugs in his pocket as the doorbell rang.

"Okay, that will be Claudia. You get yourself something to eat and go to bed. I'll see you later."

"Yes, Antonio," Beccy whispered and hung her head in submission, "You will make love to me, won't you?" she added, her voice rising to a whine

"Yes, when I get back," he replied with a sigh, but it gave him no pleasure to think about it.

The doorbell was demanding his attention, and he crossed the roam hurriedly,

"Now, you do as you're told," he said and raised his finger to her before he opened the door and disappeared.

Claudia looked in surprise when he closed the door behind him and took her arm. It was cold outside and there was a flurry of snow heralding the start of winter, and they rushed to the car.

"Beccy's not well." he said shortly and Claudia looked at him in surprise but she did not comment.

What Price Ambition?

He took her to a small bistro he sometimes used near his flat. The food was good although not very imaginative, but it was cosy and private.
Claudia listened in silence as he told her about Beccy.
"So you see, Claudia, she's really hung up. She needs my help, and I'm asking you to let me give it to her, I know it's asking more than I should, but I can't help feeling it was my fault she's in that state."
Claudia dabbed her lips delicately with the napkin., and looked at Antonio steadily,
"I've read lots of books about guys dumping their women, but I've never come across this one before. Why can't you just be honest and say you fancy her more than me, Antonio? I'd respect you more if you were honest."
"Because, that isn't true," said Antonio in frustration, "I just feel I'm the only one who can help her, and I'm asking you to wait for me."
Claudia sipped her coffee.
"Are you sleeping with her?" she said in the same monotone.
Antonio looked at her steadily, "No of course not. It's just friendship. It's you I want, Claudia."
She smiled cynically, "So, I'm what you want, Antonio. Do you love me? You've never told me."
"You know I do." protested Antonio.
Claudia shook her head, "No, I don't. I wish I did, but you've never really said anything in the least romantic

What Price Ambition?

to me. Why should I believe you, Antonio? Why won't you let me meet this girl and see for myself? Why should I wait for you? Why should I even trust you?" She put the coffee cup carefully in the saucer, and dabbed her lips again, her eyes alight like diamonds in the dim light of the restaurant.
Antonio's heart quickened.
"You're beautiful, Claudia. I do love you. I do." He repeated emphatically as if he had suddenly just realised it himself.
In fact it was not far from the truth. Up till now, he had appreciated that Claudia Ferolla was a good match for him. She was the right age, had a good background and was attractive. He liked her, and he would not find it a chore to make love to her, but he had not known her very long, and he had not had time to adjust to the idea or get to know her. She was not just a girl he fancied. She would be his wife one day, and that in itself was something special. He wanted to take their relationship slowly and find out all about her. He wanted to savour the excitement he felt growing inside him every time they met. Claudia wanted a more demonstrative relationship and he had to remain a little distant from her to stop himself getting carried away. His wife had to be a virgin on their wedding night. He would not accept any less, even if his principles were a bit outdated these days.

What Price Ambition?

"Then why don't you act as if you love me?" Claudia said, interrupting his thoughts, "We might as well be brother and sister for all the passion you show me."
Antonio lifted her left hand in his.
"Claudia, the passion I feel when I'm with you is like a raging volcano, and if it were to erupt, we would both be destroyed in its heat. It's like a fire inside me, Claudia. I can't, won't, let it get out of control, not, till we're married."
"That's silly, Antonio. I don't want to wait till we're married. It could be years."
"I don't think it's silly. You're very special, Claudia, I don't want to spoil that, and I'm sure your father wouldn't like it either if I sleep with you now. I'm sorry if you think I'm not romantic. To be honest, it's all been such a whirlwind in my life. Getting married was the last thing
on my mind, and you're right, it can't be for some time yet, Claudia, will you wear my ring and wait for me. I have to help Beccy, but I promise you she means nothing to me. Will you marry me, Claudia?"
Claudia peeled the foil off the mint chocolate slowly, her eyes firmly concentrating on what she was doing. When she had completed the task, she looked directly at Antonio.
"No, I won't marry you, Antonio. I want a man who loves me before anything else."
She saw his face crease with disappointment.

What Price Ambition?

"But I will promise you that I will wait, not for ever though. I want to get married and have babies while I'm young. If you want me, Antonio, you'll have to prove it. When I'm satisfied that you really mean it, I'll marry you, and if you're lying to me about this Beccy, you'll live to regret it... no, you'll probably die," she corrected, "My father loves me very much."
Antonio kissed her fingers, "I love you very much too, Claudia. I promise you won't regret this."
"I'd better not," she warned with a fire in her eyes, "Now, please phone my car and get him to pick me up here. I don't want to go back to your flat. We have a contract, Antonio. See that you honour it."
She got up and went to the cloakroom while Antonio paid the bill, and called her car to the restaurant.
She kissed his lips and hugged him briefly before she climbed in as the chauffeur held the door for her, and she waved slightly as it pulled away.
Antonio stood watching it as it disappeared from view, but he did not see the tears roll down Claudia's cheeks in the sanctity of the darkened car, or hear the stifled sobs which choked her as she sank back into the seat alone and unhappy.
Claudia loved Antonio with all her heart. She had wanted him from the first moment she had seen him at her Aunt Maria's birthday party, and she had been elated when her father had actually approved of her choice. He would be hers one day, but she was

What Price Ambition?

impatient. She wanted him now, all to herself, and she was hurting with jealousy that he preferred to have his friend Beccy around him.
She wiped her eyes fiercely, and tilted her chin. She would make him come to her. She would not beg. She would be faithful, even although she had declined his engagement ring, but he would have to do more than just assure her that he wanted to marry her. Antonio Agusta might be the man she wanted, but she would not throw herself at him. She closed her eyes as if to shut out her real feelings. She had made up her mind. She would wait as she had promised, but she would make sure he knew that he was not the only desirable man around.
Antonio was not the only one who could have friends of the opposite sex. She would show him.
Her resolve was strong, but somehow the task ahead was daunting, and without any real purpose. What she really wanted to do was drive to his flat, and drag that girl out. Antonio was hers, and she could not bear the thought of anyone else with him, however platonic he insisted the relationship was.

Chapter 6.

Confrontation.

It was a good thing that Claudia knew nothing of what was happening at the flat, for Antonio slept with Beccy that night and every other night they were together. He did not see Claudia before Christmas, even when he called at her
home to wish her parents compliments of the season, and take a present for Claudia. She had gone out with some friends.
He took Beccy to Glasgow for the holiday, but he drew the line at taking her home with him. Beccy sulked, but this time Antonio was firm, and refused to give in to the threats to harm herself. She tried another tack by threatening tell his Grandmother that he was sleeping with her, but she backed off when he became angry with her.
He was sorely tempted to walk away from the continual conflict, and he was weary of the constant struggle to have any life of his own. He did not mind the sex, but giving up his own freedom was becoming too high

What Price Ambition?

a price to pay. His Grandmother was as perceptive as always.

"What's wrong, Toni?" she said as he sat silently with her on Christmas Eve, seemingly wrapped up in his own thoughts.

He looked up at Anna with a start.

"It's that obvious?" he said with a cynical smile.

"To me it is. Now you just tell your Nonna what's troubling you. I'm sure it's not as bad as it seems."

"It is, Nonna. My life is in a real mess."

"Where's all that ambition? Where's the boy who was going to be the richest man in the world?"

"Lost in the great scheme of things. There are so many people trying to manipulate my life. I just don't know where it's going, Nonna."

"Then let's start at the beginning. Are you happy, Toni?"

He shook his head, "No, Nonna, I'm not."

"And what's making you unhappy? Your work, Claudia Ferolla... it's Beccy, isn't it? I told you she would bring you trouble."

"Yes, you were right, Nonna," sighed Antonio and he leaned forward with his elbows on his knees and told Anna everything.

"It doesn't give me any pleasure to say I told you so. You're not being fair to anyone, not to Claudia, not to Beccy, and least of all, not to yourself. You have to send Beccy away."

What Price Ambition?

"But she says .she'll kill herself, Nonna, I can't have that on my conscience."
Anna paused for a second so that her words would sink in. "In my experience, people like Beccy try to manipulate their victim. Let her kill herself. It's her decision in the end, but I bet she won't do it. You must stand up to her. You know that Claudia will never have you if she finds out."
"Yes, I know, Nonna, but Beccy and I don't go out much, so there's not much chance of that. It's driving me crazy. I want to see my friends. I've arranged to see Drew and Rick later but Beccy wants me to take her to a club."
Anna smiled, "You go and see the boys. I'll deal with Beccy."
She smiled at Antonio, and patted his hand, "Go on. Go now before she comes looking for you," she added.
Antonio kissed his Grandmother.
"See you later at mass, and thanks, Nonna."
When he had gone, Anna picked up the phone and spoke to Beccy. She told her that Antonio had family duties to attend to and he could not see her that night or for the next few days.
Beccy listened to Anna without saying anything, for she was slightly in awe of the regal woman who ruled the Agusta family. She liked Antonio's Grandfather, for she knew he had an eye for a pretty girl, and she thought that she could flirt with him to get her own

way. She was of course under a misapprehension, but Beccy was unaware of that. In reality, she was totally stressed out with an unfounded confidence in her own ability to succeed. She tried an attempt at blackmailing Anna too in her naivety.

"I really feel awful, Mrs. Agusta. I need to see Antonio. He knows what to do."

"Oh, I'm sure you'll manage, Beccy," said Anna calmly, "You'll have to get used to being on your own soon. We have plans for Antonio. His career, his ambitions have all been put on hold to help you. Now it's your turn to help him."

"What do you mean." said Beccy suspiciously.

"You know very well what I mean, my girl," said Anna curtly, "I know what you're trying to do, but you'll never have him. He's engaged to be married, and I want you out of his life. He won't be taking you back with him."

"Oh yes he will. I can get Antonio to do anything I want."

"We'll see about that. I'd advise you to consider your position very carefully, Beccy. Get out while you're ahead for you can't win this one."

Anna put the phone down suddenly, and turned round with a start.

"Mario!" she exclaimed, "You gave me a fright, I didn't hear you come in, old man."

What Price Ambition?

"What was that all about? Was that the girl Antonio took to London you were talking to?"
"Yes. She thinks she's got him hooked. That boy is much too caring for his own good."
"He has a soft spot like his father, Georgia. We'll soon knock that out of him, I'll see the girl."
"No, Mario, let Antonio deal with her."
"I said I would see her. Don't argue with me, woman. I won't have someone like her jeopardising the boy's future."
Anna nodded, "Very well, Mario but she's just a silly little girl. She doesn't realise what she's doing."
"Then we'll educate her. I'll go now before she gets any ideas about giving Antonio any hassle."
Mario went to the house next door, taking a bottle of malt whisky for Beccy's father. He was not a man to mince words and demanded to see Beccy straight away.
"No, I want you to stay," he said to her parents, "I want you to hear what I've got to say so that you can remind her when she forgets."
Mario stood up as Beccy entered the room, and ordered her to sit. She did not argue with the imposing man before her.
"My Antonio is a good boy. Kind, caring and compassionate, but I will not have anyone taking advantage of him. He's helped you, Beccy, given up his time and his freedom to be with you, but it has to end

What Price Ambition?

now before you destroy his life. Antonio has a great future ahead of him, but it doesn't include you, Beccy."
"Yes, it does," interrupted Beccy, "We're going to be married. We're living together now."
Mario straightened his shoulders, "My Grandson's wife will not be some scrubber who jumps into bed with him the first opportunity she gets. You will never marry Antonio. It can never be, and I'm sure he hasn't given you any indication that it might. Isn't that right?" he said sharply, raising his voice just a fraction, "Antonio has never told you he loves you, let alone ask you to marry him, has he? Answer me, girl!" he demanded.
Beccy looked at Mario sullenly, "We live together. We make love. He doesn't have to say it. Anyway, you can't talk to me like that."
Mario's eyes burned into her heart and Beccy flinched, but he ignored her remarks.
"I want you to tell Antonio that you can cope on your own now. You will not go back to London with him."
"No, I won't do that, and you can't make me." said Beccy defiantly.
Mario looked coldly at her, "I can make life more comfortable for you here," he said, controlling his anger, "What will it take, a flat in Merchant City, a car. a monthly income, a holiday for your mother and father every year in Italy. What do you want, Beccy?"
"I want Antonio. He'll take care of me."

What Price Ambition?

Her voice was a whine, pleading for compassion in her misery, but Mario merely paused for a second, and when he continued, his voice was soft, but the menacing tone was unmistakable.

"I can also make life pretty uncomfortable for you too," he said, "You will *not* see Antonio again. This time, I'm not asking you, girl. If you try to spoil things for him, I'll have to stop you."

He turned to her parents and spoke to them directly. "I think you know that I can do just that, Duncan. I hope you'll make her see sense before someone gets hurt. I've got to go and get ready for midnight mass. Merry Christmas to you."

Mario left Beccy's house, hoping that they would persuade Beccy to back off, and his advice seemed to have been taken seriously. Antonio did not hear from Beccy for several days.

The next day, after Christmas dinner with his family, Antonio phoned Claudia, but she had gone out again with a friend. Antonio was not sure he believed that. Claudia was obviously trying to avoid him. He had seen her couple of times when he was having lunch with some colleagues from the office, and once in the evening when he had left Beccy and gone out to his former haunts for an hour or two to try and get his head straight. Claudia had been with a man, and Antonio could not describe the feeling of jealousy which came over him when he saw them together. He said hello briefly, and left the club, for he could not blame her. It was not Claudia's fault they were not together, and he could not even look her in the eye, knowing that he was going home to someone else.

"She's not in," he said with a light laugh when he saw his Grandmother look questioningly at him.

"Send her some flowers, Antonio. As soon as the shops open again, you send her flowers, and say something romantic on the card. No girl can resist flowers. I think your Grandfather has something he wants to tell you. Go and walk with him. He needs the exercise, don't you old man?"

"I get enough exercise, woman, but come on, Antonio, you too, Giorgio. Leave these women to their gossiping."

The three men left the house, and walked briskly along the tree-lined avenue to the nearby park where they strolled along the edge of the pond.

"Nonna said you had something to tell me, Grandpa." said Antonio.

"I wish that woman would stop meddling," exclaimed Mario, "But yes, I have, although I didn't really want to say anything until I confirm it in a couple of days. Georgia, do you remember Francis Morrow. Well he owns an engineering company out in Australia. In the motor trade, Antonio. He's offered to look at your design."

"Offered?" said Antonio.

What Price Ambition?

"Well, I rang him and called in a favour," smiled Mario, "What's the difference? The point is, he wants you to go out there and he'll take a look. If it's any good, he wants you to work with him to develop it."

"Grandpa, that's magic. If I can get someone like Mr. Morrow to back it, I have a better chance of getting into the circuit."

"Better than a chance, Antonio," said his father, "Grandpa has also arranged for Drew to take a test drive with one of the biggest Australian formula one teams. You two can work together out there."

"But Drew's getting married next year," said Antonio, "He won't want to up stakes and leave his girl."

Mario smiled, "He won't have to. She's going with him, and her father's sponsoring Drew for a while till he gets settled. He likes the idea of a son-in-law as a Grand Prix winner."

Antonio laughed, "We're a long way from that, Grandpa, but this is great news. It's a pity Rick can't came too."

"There's nothing to stop him if he wants to go," said his father, "I'll buy his business off him. He's turned that place round nicely. You'll need a good mechanic in your team. I'm sure Grandpa can persuade Morrow to take him on too
for a short time."

What Price Ambition?

Antonio stopped and looked at both his father and his Grandfather, and then he held out both arms and hugged them both at the same time.
"This is the best day of my life," he said, but then he frowned, "I'm having problems with Beccy," he added, "I need help, Dad, Grandpa."
"All taken care of, my boy," said Mario, "That young woman won't bother you any more. I've had a word with her."
"How did you persuade her? She's been clinging to me like a limpet. I felt responsible for her, Grandpa, and I tried to help her, but she got the wrong idea, and now she won't let go. I've lost Claudia because of her."
I f
"Don't you believe it, Antonio," said Mario, Claudia won't give you up so easily. She's fighter, and she wants you. She's only playing hard to get to teach you a lesson. Don't you know anything about women? She'll come round when you've been away in Australia for a few weeks. You ask your Nonna how to keep her interest."
"Nonna's already told me," laughed Antonio, "I've got to be more romantic."
"We could teach him a thing or two, couldn't we, Giorgio?" laughed Mario.
"Too right," laughed Giorgio, "You young men don't have a clue these days."

What Price Ambition?

Antonio sent flowers to Claudia after the holiday, and dictated a message to her, which made her eyes grow bright when she read it. The brief wards came alive for her, and she heard Antonio's voice as if he was speaking to her.

".Just to say I love you," it read, and the words echoed in her head,

She telephoned him straight away, and Antonio smiled when he heard the eagerness in her voice.

"Antonio, the flowers are beautiful. Do you mean it?"

"Of course I do. I'm sorry I never told you. I just assumed... Oh hell. Claudia, I was a conceited slob, and I'm sorry. Beccy was only using me. I suppose everyone else saw it. We need to talk. I'm coming back to London tomorrow. I'll come over in the evening, that is if you still want me."

"Oh, yes," whispered Claudia, "I've never stopped wanting you."

"I don't mean like that, Claudia," said Antonio hastily, hearing the desire in her voice.

Claudia laughed, "Still the reluctant lover. I'm joking, Antonio. It's rather touching that you don't want to sully my reputation, as it were. So old- fashioned, but nice. Yes, you may come to call tomorrow evening." she mocked with a laugh.

Antonio laughed too, "You're a little witch, Claudia Ferolla, and I love you, do you hear? I'll shout it louder if you like."

What Price Ambition?

He heard her laughter tinkle like a thousand tiny bells heralding the pleasure he knew he would feel when he saw her.
"See you tomorrow, Romeo. You can tell me a thousand times."
The phone went dead, and Antonio grinned. He knew she was playing with him, stringing him out, and making him want her.
"I'll show you." he said out loud.
He had not planned to return to London till the weekend, but when he had spoken to Claudia the urge to see her was too strong, He apologised to his mother and father and went to see his Grandmother before he left,
He had no sooner got out of the car than Beccy ran into the drive, and he had to push her away firmly when she threw her arms round his neck.
"Stop it, Beccy, I'm not taken in by you any more, I know what you're playing at, I'm going back to London tomorrow to see Claudia, It's finished between us."
"No!" cried Beccy, "You can't mean that, Antonio," You love me. Let's go and make love. You'll change your mind." and she clutched desperately at his arm.
Antonio shook his head and looked at her coldly.
"You're pathetic, Beccy. I don't love you, I've never loved you, and you can't blackmail me any more. We're finished. Now, go home and get on with your life. I have other plans and it doesn't include you."

What Price Ambition?

He turned and walked away from her.
"You'll be sorry, Antonio Agusta," Beccy shouted at him, "She won't want you when she knows what you had with me. You lied to her. I'll tell her."
Antonio stopped abruptly and turned to Beccy.
"If you really love me, Beccy, you'll let me go. It can't work. I need a wife who is strong, and you need a man who can devote time to you."
Beccy stood still for a minute, and then she rushed to Antonio with tears in her eyes.
"Antonio, I need you. Please don't leave me, I can't cope without you.
Antonio held her lightly for a minute or two.
"Don't cry, Beccy. You're fine now. You've done well, and you *will* cope. You'll find someone who loves you, and you'll be happy. Be happy for me, Beccy. I am fond of you. I wouldn't have stayed with you all these months if I
wasn't."
Beccy clung to him and raised her face to his. He kissed her briefly.
"Go home, Beccy," he said softly, "I have to see, Nonna before I leave. I'm taking the early flight. I promised Claudia I would see her tomorrow night."
Beccy swallowed hard and nodded as she wiped her eyes.
"Okay, Antonio," she whispered, "Goodbye. We can still be friends, though, can't we?"

What Price Ambition?

"Sure" said Antonio, but he did not say it with any conviction, for he never wanted to see Beccy again. He left her standing there watching him go into his Grandmother's house pleased that she had at last seen sense. However he did not see the triumphant glint in Beccy's eyes behind his back. If he had, he might not have felt such relief inside him that his relationship with Beccy was over.

Mario was driving in as Beccy left, and he had to brake suddenly to avoid her.

Beccy did not seem to notice, and Mario frowned as he wound down the window to speak to her. She jumped when he spoke.

"Beccy, what brings you here?" said Mario lightly."

"I was speaking to Antonio. He's going beak to London tomorrow. He wants me to take the late flight tonight and get the flat ready for him. I told you he loved me, Mr. Agusta," she said and smiled triumphantly and walked away.

Mario's frown deepened, and he hurried into the house.

"Antonio, my boy. I've just spoken to that girl. She tells me she's going to London with you."

Antonio's smile froze instantly.

"She did what!" he exclaimed, "The little cow, I told her no such thing. What's she playing at? I'll go and sort her out once and for all."

He strode towards the door, determined to have it out with Beccy.

What Price Ambition?

"No!" ordered Mario, and Antonio stopped and went back into the room. He knew when to obey his Grandfather without question.

"Leave her to me," said Mario, "Perhaps I wasn't emphatic enough. Now, let's forget her, and have a drink to celebrate your new career. Don't worry about the bank. I've cleared it with the Chairman. You have two weeks. Just give me a minute, Antonio. I have to make a call."

Mario left Antonio with his Grandmother, and closed the door to his study before he lifted the phone.

"Nicholas, my boy, I have a job for you."

Beccy had only just closed the door when the phone rang, and her mother called her to take the call. It was Nicholas Derwent.

"Hi Beccy," he said pleasantly, "I heard you were back. I've missed you, Darling. I'd like to see you. I'll pick you up in fifteen minutes."

Beccy hesitated and then smiled as she answered him. "Why not. It will be nice to renew old friendships, but I'm leaving for London later, Nicholas. We won't have much time together."

Nicholas laughed, "It won't take long, Darling. I've got a real hard on just thinking about you."

Beccy laughed with excitement. Nicholas was always good to her. They had fun together, and she missed that. He was there in fifteen minutes as he promised, and he swung Beccy off her feet when she opened the door.

What Price Ambition?

"Come on, Darling, I've got some real good stuff. Let's cut it and chill out. I haven't had a good lay since you left with that poser, Agusta. He's a loser, Beccy. Stick with me if you want to hit the high spots."
Beccy laughed and took his arm.
"You always know what turns me on, Nicholas." she said softly, as they went out to his car.
When he brought her home again, Beccy was high on cocaine and hooked once more. He phoned Mario from his mobile phone before he drove away from Beccy's house.
"Nicholas here, Boss. She'll be no more trouble. Give me a week and she won't even be around to cause you any more grief."
"Good, Nicholas. Your next delivery will have a little bonus in it."
However, Nicholas had not reckoned with the single-minded determination which drove Beccy. She lay on her bed for a couple of hours, spaced out with the drugs and dreaming of Antonio. Then when she came down a little, she packed a bag, left a note for her parents, and went to the airport to catch a flight to London. She still had the keys to Antonio's flat so it was no problem. Once there, she crossed the hall table, and looked at the buttons on the phone. Antonio had neatly recorded every name he had stored on the memory, and Beccy smiled when her finger stopped at Claudia's name. She wiped her hair from her forehead, and the perspiration

What Price Ambition?

made her hand damp. She started to breath faster and shallower. She did not feel well, and she sat down heavily.
She was suddenly tired, and her vision was blurred as she tentatively touched the key pad with a shaky finger. She intended speaking to Claudia Ferolla to tell her that Antonio was living with her. She jumped with a start when a man's voice answered. It was a voice she recognised and a wave of fear washed over her, It was Mario Agusta. She slammed the phone down in a panic, not knowing what to do, but then she took a deep breath and looked at the directory again. She had pushed the wrong button in her drug induced state.
The one she wanted was the one immediately under it. It took only a second for her to redial, and Beccy waited impatiently for Claudia to answer. However she was out of luck for Claudia was not at home.
While Beccy was redialling the correct number, Mario was seething with anger.
He had recognised Beccy's voice, even from the few words she spoke, and he knew that something was not quite right. On impulse, he dialled the recall code, and the announcement told him that the call had been made from Antonio's flat. He knew that Antonio had not yet left for London, and suddenly he thumped the table.
"What is it, Mario?" said Anna.
"That girl has gone to Antonio's flat in London. She's out to cause him trouble if I'm not mistaken. I thought

What Price Ambition?

Derwent had taken care of her. Well, this time she will *not* succeed."
"Mario what are you going to do? She's only a child. Antonio wouldn't want you to hurt her."
"Keep out of this woman. She will *not* stand in Antonio's way."
He picked up the phone again, and had a brief conversation before he joined Anna in the sitting room. "Don't worry. My people will help her to see where her future lies."
The man Mario had called was one of his lieutenants in London, and as soon as Mario had given the order he put the wheels of their organisation into motion.
Beccy was asleep when the lock on the door was expertly forced, and two men slid silently into the hall. She was an easy target for the two, highly trained operatives, and they quickly put a chloroform soaked cloth over her face until she was unconscious. Then they carried her limp form out of the flat and into a car with tinted windows. From there, they took her to a private jet, and flew her back to Glasgow. The city centre hotel to which they transferred her had a reputation for dubious clientele, and they were not questioned when they carried Beccy inside. Before they left her, they injected her with a lethal dose of almost pure cocaine, and left the syringe with further supplies beside the bed.

What Price Ambition?

In the morning, when the maid found Beccy, she was dead. The police were called, but to them, it seemed perfectly straight forward. Their brief enquiries revealed that she was a drug user. They even suspected that she could be a pusher. It was no surprise that she had used cocaine once too often, not knowing that the supply was unusually pure. Their theory was collaborated by the porter who confirmed that he had booked Beccy in like any other guest. He was well paid for his co-operation, and knew very well where his loyalties lay, for he had helped them out before.
The case of Beccy Roberts, drug addict was filed and closed.

What Price Ambition?

Chapter 7.

The Betrothal.

Antonio returned to London unaware of what was happening to Beccy. He had Claudia on his mind, and plans to woo her like the old-fashioned Romeo she had called him.

He went shopping before he went home, and when he called at the Ferolla house in the evening, he was carrying a huge box. The guards at the entrance made him open it even although they knew him, but they smiled and joked with him when they saw the contents. Claudia could not even see his face when he carried it into the room where he set it down and bowed to her.

"Not Romeo and Juliette but Antonio and Claudia. Good evening Mrs.Ferolla. You look as beautiful as ever. Your daughter obviously takes after you."

"Oh Antonio, you're such a charmer," said Mrs. Ferolla. Whatever have you got in that box?"

"Open it," he said to Claudia, and she smiled as she laughed and undid the ribbon.

What Price Ambition?

A heart shaped balloon rose into the air and she laughed again with pleasure.
On the balloon was painted a red heart and a card hung underneath.
Claudia looked at Antonio in amazement.
"Read the card," he said, and she read it out loud.
"Cupid's arrow has pierced my heart, and I love you, Claudia. Pierce the heart on the balloon and I'll prove it to you. Forever, Antonio."
Claudia pulled the pin which was attached to the card and stuck it in the balloon which immediately shrivelled and fell to the floor with a thump.
Claudia picked up the remnant and took out the box which was visible, and opened it.
"Antonio!" she shrieked with delight, "It's beautiful."
"It sparkles like your eyes. Will you marry me, Claudia?"
He took the box from her hands and picked out the diamond ring.
Claudia smiled at him and her face had a mischievous twist as she looked at him under her dark hair.
"Very good, Antonio," she said softly, "But I don't think Romeo would do it like that."
Antonio hesitated and frowned, his temper rising at the bait.
"Claudia stop teasing the boy." said her mother.
"It's alright, Mrs. Ferolla," said Antonio with a grin, "She's right."

What Price Ambition?

He leaped over the back of the couch and plucked some flowers from a vase on a table behind Claudia, and got down on one knee in front of her.
He held the flowers up to her, but Claudia screeched.
"You're dripping water everywhere, Antonio!"
"What price true love," he said dramatically, "I offer you my heart, and you complain about a little water. Claudia, take my heart and keep it safe, for it's no longer mine. I am yours, sweet Claudia. Will you marry me, and make me the happiest man in the world?"
"Oh yes, Antonio," she laughed, "I love you. You make a wonderful Romeo."
He slipped the ring on her finger and kissed her.
"Now then, where's the champagne?" he whispered and nibbled her ear.
'Is that all you can think of," she whispered back, "Antonio my mother is watching us."
"Then let's go somewhere private. I have something to tell you."
She pushed him away, "Mum, do you think we could have champagne to celebrate?" she said, and smiled with satisfaction when her mother volunteered to phone Dimitri first so that they could all celebrate.
"I thought she would never go. Antonio, kiss me."
She pulled him savagely towards her, and Antonio felt the hairs on his neck prickle.
"Hey, don't get me all fired up," he whispered, "I'm still not going to sleep with you till we're married."

What Price Ambition?

Claudia turned away from him, her lips pouting in a sulk.
"Antonio, that's silly. No-one waits these days."
"Well, maybe we'll start a new fashion."
"You can't do this to me. Maybe I'll find someone who's willing, Antonio Agusta."
Antonio turned sharply from the window.
"I don't want you to so much as smile at another guy," he said, and Claudia saw the smouldering passion in his eyes."
"I'm not your possession," she snapped at him, "I'll do whatever I want."
"Not as my fiancée, you won't. That's one thing I'm really hung up on. From now on, you're my woman, and I'll break anyone's neck who so much as looks at you the wrong way. Do you understand, Claudia?"
"Yes, Antonio," she said meekly, "I'm sorry, I was only joking."
"Well don't joke about that," he said curtly, "You're the only love in my life and I expect you to feel the same way."
"Oh I do, Antonio," said Claudia quickly, "But I don't want to be something you own. Antonio, what do you really want me for?"
Claudia moved to his side, and put her arm through his, "Do you want me because you fell in love with me, and find me irresistible, or is it because my father and your Grandfather have agreed a marriage contract?"

What Price Ambition?

Antonio did not answer her immediately, and Claudia rested her head on his shoulder.
"Is it me you want, Antonio, or the power which comes with me?"
Antonio took the hand which now wore his ring, and he kissed her fingers before he looked directly at her.
"Grandpa was negotiating a contract before I was ready. I liked you and I told him as much, but I wasn't sure then if I was really in love with you, Claudia. I wouldn't marry you if I didn't love you. I've had enough of pretence."
He broke off, for he was just about to tell her about Beccy.
Claudia looked up at him with large trusting eyes.
"What pretence? You're talking in riddles, Antonio. I thought you said you would always be open and honest with me."
"I am, Claudia, I've never told you anything but the truth about what I feel for you. It wasn't you."
He hesitated, and then he took a deep breath, coming to a decision.
"Claudia, I don't want to start our relationship with a lie. We have to be totally honest with one another. I was sleeping with Beccy. I had to. She was crazy. I was afraid she would kill herself. I'm sorry. I shouldn't have lied to
you."

What Price Ambition?

"No, you shouldn't," said Claudia softly, "But it's alright, Antonio, I know."
She took Antonio completely by surprise, and he let go her hand.
"You knew! How?"
Claudia smiled, "You don't think that Dimitri would let his beloved daughter marry anyone without first checking them out. I told my father I wanted to know everything he found out about you. Your bedroom was bugged."
"Bugged!" exclaimed Antonio in disbelief, "That's real scary stuff."
"I'm sure your Grandfather, Dom Mario has checked me out just as thoroughly. Antonio, for someone who's going to inherit from Dom Mario, you're very naive. I had to provide medical records, did you know that?"
"This is incredible. I had no idea they interfered so much,. Do you mean that they would have stopped us marrying if your pedigree didn't come up to scratch?"
Claudia laughed again, and she grabbed Antonio's hands with a deep twinkle in her eyes.
"No, probably not, if you really wanted me, but not being a virgin or being unable to have children would have been a problem."
"But what if we had slept together? You might have slept with me before we get married, but that doesn't make you promiscuous, so how could they tell."

What Price Ambition?

"Antonio, you really are so innocent. No of course it doesn't, silly, but you would have been told and given the choice of accepting me. You've jumped the gun by proposing to me before they got round to the formalities.

"Would you?" she said curiously, "Would you still want me if I had been sleeping with someone else?"
Antonio answered her without hesitation.
"Not as my wife, but I'd still want you, You turn me on like crazy."
Claudia tossed her head and turned away from him.
"That's not the answer I expected."
"Come on, Claudia, it's irrelevant. You've not been with anyone else. I could tell that the first time we met, so the question never arose. Why didn't you dump me when you found out about Beccy?"
Claudia shrugged, "I wouldn't want a man who wasn't experienced, and it's acceptable for men to have affairs. My father knew you were being discreet to protect me, and he respected you for that. I knew you didn't love her. I was

jealous though," she said suddenly, and turned round sharply, "And you needn't think I'll tolerate it when we're married. You'll be mine then, and I'm not going to share you with anyone. I hope that's clear, Antonio."
"Yes, ma'am," laughed Antonio, "Just the two of us together, I've got no complaints about that, just as long as you keep me happy."

What Price Ambition?

He held her round her waist and kissed her fiercely till she relaxed completely in his arms. As she pressed close to him, he pushed her backwards and laid her on the couch, sliding his hand fervently over her tight shirt and jeans.

"Just let me touch you," he whispered, and he undid the buttons on her shirt to push his fingers inside the fabric. The softness of her breasts inside the lace he felt made him tingle with a warm glow from the tip of his toes to his neck.

"Oh god, Antonio," whispered Claudia, "That feels, so, so electric. Oh please don't, not here. Mum will be back in a minute." she added with a soft whine, half pleading with him to stop and half anticipating the thrill.

Antonio ignored her, and removed his hand from her breasts to slide it down her jeans and between her thighs, making her jump when an involuntary convulsion shot a river of pleasure through her. She held him tightly, her
breath fast and hot against his cheek, and her body tense with desire.

"That's just a taste of things to come," Antonio whispered and got up.

"I hate you, Antonio," Claudia said and sat up, her face tinged pink with excitement.

"I think you're beautiful," said Antonio softly, his eyes locked on the roundness of her breasts, heaving and just visible inside the shirt which was still undone.

What Price Ambition?

Claudia suddenly became aware of the direction of his gaze, and hastily buttoned her shirt.

"You can't get me wound up like that and then drop me," she whispered, "It's so frustrating, Antonio."

"I'm sorry, Sweetheart." he said and sat down on the couch beside her.

Her lips parted slightly at his nearness, and she looked at him with tenderness radiating from her eyes.

"You've never called me that before. It's the first time you've ever used any term of endearment."

"You are my Sweetheart, and I love you. Give me time. I have to get used to being in love. It's all a bit strange, and I can't help wondering if I'm dreaming."

"Let's not wait too long, Antonio. I'll be eighteen next month and Dad will let me marry then."

Antonio took her hand and turned the diamond ring on her finger,

"I can't Claudia," he said, and he could not look at her, "That's what I wanted to talk you about. I'm going to Australia for a while."

"Australia!" said Claudia as if it was a word she had not heard before, "Don't be silly, Antonio. What would you do in Australia?"

Antonio dropped her hand suddenly as if he had been scalded and got up.

She saw the anger in his eyes,

"I'm neither silly nor incapable of sorting out my own life, Claudia, and don't treat me like some plaything

What Price Ambition?

your father bought to amuse you. I'm going to Australia to work with a company which is prepared to develop my engine. My friends, Rick and Drew are coming too. We'll have our own formula one team one day, and in the meantime, we'll
all be working to develop out skills and experience."
"Antonio, you can't" wailed Claudia, "I won't see you for months. I might never see you."
"Don't be so dramatic, Claudia. It won't be for a while, but
that's not such a bad thing. You've got a lot of growing up to do, Claudia. I don't want a spoiled little Daddy's girl for a wife. I have plans, and it might not always be what *you* want."
"But a factory worker!" said Claudia in disgust,
"Grease and dirt. You have a nice office job, and it pays well. What do you know about factories anyway?"
"I've built engines ever since I can remember, and don't be
such a snob, Claudia. A little honest dirt won't make me a worse person."
"I don't want to be married to a factory worker. Dad don't let him go!" she cried as her father came into the room,
"Calm down Claudia," said Dimitri, "What have you done to upset my little girl, Antonio?"

What Price Ambition?

"I was just telling her that I'm not a puppet, Mr. Ferolla. I'm going to Australia to work and Claudia doesn't like it."

He told Dimitri his plans.

"You see, Dad," said Claudia, "Don't you think it's a silly idea?"

"No, I don't," said Dimitri, "If that's what Antonio wants to do, he should do it now while he's young. Go for it, my boy. You'll never know what you can do if you don't try."

Claudia could not believe her ears. Her father was agreeing with Antonio against her wishes.

"Dad, I won't be able to see him. Make him change his mind."

"Enough, Claudia. Antonio's man enough to decide for himself. It won't hurt you to wait for him, and prepare for your marriage. There's your house to build, your mother will teach you to cook. Now where is that ring your mother tells me Antonio gave you like a true Italian."

"I'm not going to cook!" said Claudia, "He can employ someone to do that."

Claudia stopped her ranting abruptly when she saw Antonio's eyes. He was looking at her strangely, like someone he had never seen before.

"I think we have a lot to discuss before we get married," he said quietly, "I suggest you take cooking lessons while I'm away, Claudia. It will keep you out of mischief. There won't be any cook in *my* house. It was good enough for my Mother and my Grandmother, and your Mother too for that matter, so I think you should follow their example. Now, I'm going home. It's been a-long day, and quite revealing I think. I'll see you tomorrow, but I'll be later. There's something I have to do first."

"But, Antonio." began Claudia.

"Goodnight, Claudia," Antonio interrupted and kissed her cheek, "Goodnight, Mrs. Ferolla, Mr. Ferolla."

Dimitri was smiling after he had walked with Antonio to the door.

"I like that boy. He'll make a good husband for you, Claudia. He lets you know who will be boss in his family."

"I don't like him any more," Claudia blurted out, "He only wants me to work and slave in his house."

"Oh I think he wants you for more than that, my girl." laughed Dimitri, "That's a nice ring he gave you."

Claudia pulled at the ring in frustration, but it would not come off, and she gave up.

"I can't wait for years," she said, her eyes pleading with her father, "I'll be so lonely without him. He doesn't want me to go out with anyone else."

"I should hope not, my girl. A Family betrothal is not to be taken lightly. It won't be years if I know Antonio. He's got his head screwed on, that young man. He'll make it work for him, and he'll be home in no time.

What Price Ambition?

You could always make your home with him in Australia, Claudia."
Claudia looked at her father in horror.
"No way. I draw the line at that. If that's what he's planning, he can forget me. I'm not going to live in Australia miles from everyone."
Antonio was tired when he got home, and intended going straight to bed.
However, he stopped at the bedroom door. The duvet was trailing on the floor, and the pillows ruffled as if someone had got out of it in a hurry. He knew that he and Beccy had left it neatly made when they left before Christmas, and he looked around uneasily. Claudia's words came back to him, If her father's man could get in without his knowing, so could others. He checked the other rooms but nothing was out of place there, and he returned to the bedroom. He wandered around it for a few minutes puzzled by what he had found, and then he sat down on the bed. He stared at the millions of stars in the sky through the window and as the moon suddenly cast light on to the dressing table, his eyes were drawn downwards. There was an electric razor there, a man's razor, but it was not his. It was Beccy's. He had teased her about it when he had seen her using it on her legs, but now it was no laughing matter. Beccy had packed that razor when she had left with him. She must have returned to the flat, but where was she? He looked in the bathroom, but there was nothing there belonging to

What Price Ambition?

Beccy, and on impulse, he went to the phone and dialled Beccy's number.

"Hello, I'd like to speak to Beccy. It's Antonio." he said when Beccy's mother answered.

There was silence at the other end, and then a sob.

"What is it?" said Antonio as the woman burst into uncontrollable sobbing.

Then Beccy's father was on the line, and he heard her mother tell him who was calling.

"Antonio," said Beccy's father, and Antonio heard his voice crack with emotion. He went on.

"You obviously don't know. Beccy's dead. She was found in a hotel room here. She had overdosed on cocaine. It's funny. She told her mother she was going to London to be with you. Did she contact you?"

Antonio shook his head, struck dumb at the news, and then he remembered they could not see him.

"No, I haven't heard from her. I'm sorry. I thought she was off the stuff. She promised," he said in a daze.

"We thought so too, but she was very upset when your Grandfather told her to stay away from you. She was in love with you."

"No, she wasn't," said Antonio, hastily, for he did not want to shoulder any of the blame for her death, "She needed someone to lean on, to be with her all the time. I couldn't give her that, and I didn't love her. I told her so."

"Well she's dead, whatever was in her head at the time."

What Price Ambition?

"I'm sorry," said Antonio again and abruptly put the phone down.
He felt the burden of guilt even if it was not directly his fault. If he had been there with her, he could have stopped her. He knew in his heart that Beccy would never really have been stable. It might have been possible to prevent her this time, but there would have been a next and a next. Beccy was a loser. Bright, vulnerable little Beccy, but still a loser. Nicholas Derwent had seen to that. He saw Derwent's sneer in his mind, and he knew he had something to do with it.
"I'll kill the bastard!" he said out loud.
He went back to the bedroom and caught sight of the razor again.
"She was here," he said to himself, "But why did she leave?"
Then it hit him like a blow to the gut.
Beccy had been taken from his flat by force. His mind raced desperately. Derwent! No, he did not have the connections to organise something like that.
Dimitri Ferolla. No, he would not have known Beccy was in the flat. He was not expecting Antonio till the next day, today. Who else would have known? Her parents, Why would they?.. His mind suddenly froze. His Grandfather! He had seen Beccy, spoken to her. He had the resources, the authority and the motive.
"The bastard!" hissed Antonio fiercely, "I won't forgive him if he's had Beccy murdered."

What Price Ambition?

He shook his head to clear out the evil thoughts there. His Grandfather would never lay that on him. He might twist her arm a bit and persuade her to leave, but the murder of his friend. He could not believe that Mario was so vindictive. Beccy could not have been any threat to anyone except herself, but maybe she had tried to blackmail Mario like she had done with him. Mario was a different kettle of fish. He was ruthless, even Nonna said so. His Grandmother"! Maybe Anna would know the truth, he would speak to her in the morning.
Antonio hardly slept that night. He had liked Beccy, enjoyed her company in the beginning, and had got a lot of satisfaction from making love to her. He had not loved her, but he had been very fond of her, and he had never wanted her hurt. Now she was dead, and it *was* his fault.
The encouragement he had given her right at the start had made her believe that their relationship had a future, but he had left her to further his career in London. Beccy had needed him, and because he was not there, Nicholas
Derwent had won her heart with his charm, his money and his drugs. Beccy did not understand men like Derwent, and she had been an easy target for him to get her hooked and use her in his drug trafficking.
Beccy had coped well in London, and, if Antonio ignored her possessive grasp on his life, they had not

had a bad time together. If he had not met Claudia, he would have been happy enough to live with Beccy. He should not have abandoned her at Christmas. She was not ready to go it alone, yet she had seemed reconciled to the fact that she could not have him. Why had she changed her mind? Why had she been killed? He could not bear to think about it, and he woke up sweating.
He got up and made himself some coffee. The hot liquid flowed through his body like something inside him searching for the right thoughts, but when they formed in his mind, he was not sure he wanted to deal with it.
He had accepted the benevolence of his Grandfather, and the responsibilities which accompanied being heir to the Agusta empire. Perhaps that had been a mistake. He suspected that Mario was responsible for Beccy's death, but he could not understand why. Mario had told him he had persuaded Beccy to back off, so there should not have been any need to take it further. Something must have happened.
Antonio knew Beccy had been in his flat. He had forgotten about the key still in her possession. She had been in his bed, the bed they had shared, and she would have known that he would be back today. She must have been planning to come between him and Claudia. Even so, Mario still had no reason to kill her.

What Price Ambition?

Antonio finished his coffee, and stared at the bottom of the empty cup. He was assuming a great deal, and suspecting his Grandfather when he had no real proof. As he sat in the lonely kitchen, his elbows resting on the breakfast bar, he frowned and the creases in his brow spread to the corners of his mouth. Suddenly, he threw the empty cup across the room, and watched it shatter against the wall.

He was angry. His Grandfather had no right to interfere, let alone make a monumental decision like that for him. He would tell him the deal was off in the morning. If this was what being heir to the Family business meant, he did not want it.

Antonio frowned again. If the deal was off, it would have far reaching consequences. His marriage to Claudia, his trip to Australia, his friends, Drew and Rick. It could jeopardise the future for them all. It would certainly ruin his plans. He would have no future in the motor racing world, not now, not ever, for they would not trust him again.

Antonio thumped the table.

"Fuck!" he said out loud, "Fuck Grandpa, fuck Beccy!"

He knew he could not pull out now. He would have to ignore all this if he wanted the things he had set his heart on, but he was not sure if he could just go on as if nothing had happened. He had to speak to his Grandmother. She would know what to do.

What Price Ambition?

First though, he had to search for the spy cameras in his apartment. It was no easy task and when a manual search produced nothing, he left the apartment to find some help. Later he returned with the latest in bug detection equipment and when he swept the apartment again, he found four small devices placed in light fittings. He also taped up the web cam on his laptop and unplugged his television. Satisfied that Dimirti could no longer spy on him, he went back to bed and this time to fall asleep into a deep but restless slumber, where dragons and monsters jumped out at him wherever he turned.

In the morning, he felt drained, but he got up and went to work at the bank. There were still two weeks to go with them, but his heart was not in it this morning. Ralph Beaton was smug and annoying, and he took pains to make it clear that they all knew Antonio was leaving.

"Can't stand the heat, old chap?" said Beaton, "I hear you're going to be working in a factory. That's probably more your style anyway."

"No-one asked you, Beaton," said Antonio, and he turned back to his computer screen and carried on working.

Beaton laughed, "I don't need your permission, Agusta. I'm pleased for you. Really... and for us of course. We won't have to put up with your insufferable attitude.

What Price Ambition?

Not all of us enjoy privileges from our family. Some of us do it on merit."

Antonio turned round sharply, swinging the swivel chair so violently that it toppled over when he sprang at Beaton. He hit him hard in the gut, and then on the edge of the jaw on the way down.

"Here's something you can have on merit, Beaton, and you're lucky that I don't kill you."

"Mr. Agusta!" said the manager, who had been summoned, "Leave the floor at once!"

"Don't worry, I intend to. I'm sorry, I won't be back. I don't think I'm welcome here."

He looked around at the people who had been his colleagues in the past few months, and his gaze rested on Francesca. He smiled at her and she returned the smile and blew him a kiss.

"I've enjoyed working with most of you, and despite what some of you might think, I do appreciate the help you gave me. It won't be forgotten. I'm sorry it had to end like this, but c'est la vie, my friends," he grinned, "Look out for my name in lights. I'll hit the headlines one day. Ciaou."

He did not even bother to clear his desk. They could throw it all away, for he would not need it again.

It was a short walk from the office to the nearby cafe, and Antonio walked briskly. He sat and read the newspapers with a cup of coffee for a while until he

What Price Ambition?

was sure that his Grandfather would be out. Then he went to his apartment and phoned his Grandmother. Anna was reluctant to discuss it, and Antonio frowned. She seemed to be making excuses for Mario.
"Nonna, all I want is for you to tell me if I'm right. Did Grandpa have Beccy killed?"
"Antonio, what sort of question is that?" said Anna with a nervous laugh, "Why would Mario want to do that?"
"You tell me, Nonna. I've got to know. I'll never forgive him if he did,. You know that don't you."
Antonio heard Anna sigh softly before she replied.
"No, I didn't know, My Toni," she said, "The time has come. I want you to take the next plane home."
"Why, Nonna?" said Antonio, his heart suddenly pounding like a violent storm in his chest, "You sound so strange, Nonna. What is it?"
"Just come home, Antonio. No, on second thoughts, don't come here. I'll come to you. I'll phone you from the airport, and you can pick me up."
She put down the phone suddenly, and left Antonio looking in amazement at the handset.
His Grandmother had always been special for him. She was someone he could always turn to, and who always had time for him. She was a remarkable woman, and she never ceased to amaze him.
In some ways, Claudia reminded him of her. They were both highly opinionated, and in control of their lives. They were both excitable, yet at the same time, soft and

What Price Ambition?

feminine. They both loved him. He smiled at the thought. His Grandmother approved of Claudia, and that was important to him.

What Price Ambition?

Chapter 8.

The Casket.

Antonio was like a caged lion for the rest of the day till he met Anna at the airport and drove her back to the flat.
"Antonio, you'll get a speeding ticket." she complained as he darted in and out of the traffic.
Antonio laughed, "They'll have to catch me first."
He put his foot down, "I'll show you driving, Nonna."
"Now you can make me some tea," said Anna as she flopped down on the couch, "You'll give me a heart attack."
Antonio smiled, "Not you, Nonna. You're too tough for anything like that. Tea coming up for my favourite girl."
Antonio made the tea and put it down in front of Anna "Now, what's the mystery, Nonna?" he said, bursting with curiosity.

What Price Ambition?

"All in good time, Antonio. First you tell me what happened. Every detail now. I want to be sure."
Antonio looked at his Grandmother trying to read her thoughts, but she was giving nothing away, so he told her what he had found when he returned to the flat.
"Is it true, Nonna? Would Grandpa do that to Beccy?"
Anna sipped her tea, and did not look at Antonio for some seconds which hung in the air like an invisible balloon. At last she sighed and put the cup down carefully, leaning forward to take Antonio's hand.
"Bring me the box," she said softly.
Antonio knew at once what she meant, and quickly fetched the casket Anna had given him.
"Take it out."
"What's it for, Nonna? What door does it unlock?"
"The door to happiness and to sadness too." she added cryptically.
She settled back in the couch.
"Sit down, Antonio and I'll tell you about the key.
Antonio sat down, his heart beating faster, for he knew he was about to discover his Grandmother's secret.
Anna began.
"I was young like Claudia once," she said and she smiled wistfully, "And in love too."
"With Grandpa?"
Anna smiled but she shook her head, "No, not with Mario."
Antonio looked at her sharply, and she went on.

What Price Ambition?

"I fell in love with the son of a local landowner, and he loved me too, but when we met, he was already married. His name was Antonio, just like yours.
Mario was the son of our Don, also very powerful. He wanted me to marry him, and for a while, before I really knew Antonio, I saw Mario a great deal. He was very handsome and exciting, and everywhere we went he got what he wanted.
People were afraid of his father. Then, his father died and Mario became head of the family, the Don. He was only twenty, and too young to appreciate the responsibilities of such an important position, He was also very busy, and was away a lot. Antonio came back to the village for good when his wife died tragically. We met again at her funeral, and he came to my father's restaurant every night after that. We fell in love, and both families were happy with the union. The wedding day was set, the middle of June among the roses, but Mario returned two days before. He was very angry and threatened Antonio. He said I was his woman, but he had no claim on me. There was no betrothal, no contract, not even an understanding. I was angry too, and I told Mario that I was going to Antonio to be married. He ordered my father to keep me in the house, and said he would deal with Antonio. I had to see him and warn him. No- one else would help Antonio. They were too afraid of Mario. I climbed out of my bedroom window, and jumped to the ground. I hurt my ankle, but

What Price Ambition?

I didn't feel it at the time. I ran to Antonio's house, and got there before Mario. He was so sure of himself that he went for a drink first with his friends.
Antonio and I ran away and hid in a small cottage on his father's estate. Next day we were married secretly."
Anna hesitated, and looked directly at Antonio.
"We made love together that first night. Antonio was my first and only love. I loved him with all my heart."
Antonio saw the tears of sorrow in her eyes, and crossed the floor to sit beside her on the couch.
"What happened, Nonna?" he said quietly.
Anna choked back a sob, "Even after all these years it's still painful, Antonio. Mario and his men found us on our wedding night, just before dawn. He had Antonio shot in the bed beside me. I saw his eyes, Antonio. There was no remorse or guilt. He was ruthless, a man without heart. My Antonio died in my arms, and my heart went with him."
"Nonna this is awful but how could you live with him?"
"Yes, it was. For months I was numb with the shock. Mario had the priest destroy our marriage records, just as if it had never happened. I married Mario a week after Antonio's death. I didn't care what happened to me.
He was always very gentle with me and gave me everything I wanted, but of course I didn't want anything from him. When your father was born, he brought me great happiness, and that was something

What Price Ambition?

Mario could never take from me. You see, Antonio, your father was not Mario's child, he was Antonio's. He has a family birthmark on his right thigh, just as you do."
"You mean, Mario isn't my Grandfather."
"No, your real Grandfather was my beloved Antonio. Only his sister knows now because their father is dead. I've never told another living soul. Your father, Giorgio, had a half sister, Antonio's child by his first wife. They never knew one another. I don't know what happened to her."
"And the key. Nonna?"
Anna picked up the key, "The key opens the door to the chapel on your Great-Grandfather's estate in Italy. He knew the truth right from the beginning, and had the chapel closed as a shrine to Antonio. He was buried there. The old man willed everything to your father when he was still a baby. It's still in trust for him, and it will be yours one day, Antonio. It's a proud family, and they're waiting to welcome you back. You will also find there next to Antonio's tomb, a small brass plaque under which is buried papers for my marriage to Antonio, and your father's real birth certificate. I had him registered correctly and the original papers are in the tomb."
"That's quite a story, Nonna. So why didn't you leave Grandpa... Mario, when you could?"
"I had nowhere to hide. He was Don. He would not allow me to leave and I had my children. I knew that

What Price Ambition?

Mario would have no compassion if it was something he wanted. I'm telling you this because he knew that Beccy would be difficult to manipulate, and he did not want anything to come between you and Claudia. He *is* very fond of you, Antonio."

Antonio got up, "The bastard!" was all he could utter, "He'll pay for this. I never wanted this, Nonna, and if that's what being Don is about, he can keep it."

Anna caught his hand.

"Come and sit down," she said softly, "I haven't finished yet."

Antonio returned to the couch and sat silently for a few minutes as Anna started to speak again.

"There's something else the key unlocks, Antonio, metaphorically speaking. In the casket along with my marriage papers, there's a handkerchief soaked with Antonio's blood. It was the one I used to wipe his face before he died. That night I cut my own finger as Antonio lay dead beside me, and as my blood mixed with his, I vowed to avenge his death. The handkerchief is tied with a

lock of hair from Antonio and from me. I want you to go to Tuscany, Antonio and bring back the promise I made for the vendetta against Mario."

Antonio stared at his Grandmother, for he knew what that meant.

"You mean arrange his death, kill Mario,"

What Price Ambition?

"You must kill him," whispered Anna, "All these years I've hated that man, and waited, Oh yes, I've waited. Waited for the right moment. When you were born, Antonio, the setting sun shone through your nursery window like a river of blood across your forehead. I knew then that you would be the one. You will avenge your Grandfather and me. You will kill Mario Agusta."
Antonio shook his head, "No I can't, Nonna. I couldn't kill anyone, not even Mario."
Anna looked steadily at Antonio.
"Just imagine for a moment that Mario had taken a dislike to Claudia instead of Beccy, What if he had killed Claudia because *he* didn't want you to marry her?"
Anna did not go on, for she saw Antonio's face darken.
"He wouldn't dare," he said quietly, "Not someone I really care about."
"Don't you believe it," said Anna scornfully, "Your father, Giorgio, was never allowed to marry the girl he wanted. She was a Bertini, and you know how Mario hates that family. Your father married your mother when the Bertini girl was sent to Italy. Neither family wanted the match and they came to an agreement. Mario came out of it very well. He acquired the northeast of the city."
"You're not telling me that it's all down to money, Nonna."

What Price Ambition?

"Antonio, surely you're not that naive," said Anna sharply, "Of course it is. Mario will do very well out of your marriage contract with Claudia."
"I don't believe this!" exploded Antonio, "It's like something medieval. What if I just take Claudia and move to the other side of the world?"
"He'll find you," said Anna simply, "You have to honour your contract with him. Everything from now on is negotiated round you as his heir. He won't let you forget it, and sooner or later the independence you value will have disappeared. You'll become another Mario Agusta, just as he did when he took over from his father and his father did the same before him."
"Never! Why didn't Dad take it on?"
"He was a broken boy after Mario's interference with his love for the Bertini girl. He lost his heart to her, and he just gave up after that. He could never take on Mario. He was like me. He just accepted his fate, but you're different
Antonio. You have your Grandfather's spirit. You must stop him."
"No Nonna!" said Antonio emphatically, "I'm not going to have a murder on my conscience for you or anyone else."
"But you already have," said Anna softly, "Beccy died because of you."

What Price Ambition?

Anna's words hit him like a knife through his heart. His Grandmother had never before said anything to hurt him.
"That's not fair, Nonna," he protested, "I never wanted her dead. I could have handled her."
"But you left it to Mario. You didn't bother to ask him how he would get rid of her, did you?" persisted Anna
Antonio was seeing a side to his Grandmother he had not suspected existed. She was making him feel guilty for his part in Beccy's death, and he hung his head.
"No, I didn't. I suppose you're right. I *am* responsible." he said.
Anna patted his hand, "I don't want you to get hung up about it. I'm only trying to tell you that you're involved in Mario's schemes whether you like it or not. The only way to make your own mark is to take over."
Antonio sat down abruptly, and put his head in his hands.
"I can't, Nonna. I'm obviously not the man you think I am. I don't hate him that much. He's always been my Grandpa. It's your vendetta, Nonna."
"Don't you care that he's deprived you of your birthright?" Antonio shook his head, "No, I don't know these people you've talked about. My life was in Glasgow where I was brought up, not Italy. I'm sorry, Nonna, I won't do it."
"I'm disappointed Antonio," but then she smiled, "But I'm glad you've not inherited Mario's character as well

as his business, Very well, Antonio, I won't hold you to your promise. Your father doesn't know anything, I've never told him because he couldn't handle it. Neither does Mario, so you can't claim your Italian inheritance while he's alive. He would never allow it."

"But how can he stop me or rather, my father if we're entitled to, it?"

Anna laughed bitterly, "Toni, you're so naive. Mario has never known that Giorgio is not his eldest son, If he were to find out, he would be devastated. He would disinherit both of you publically. You would no longer be part of this family. Dimitri Ferolla would not want you to marry his daughter. Although, your Italian connections might count for something."

"And don't I count for anything? You're all playing your games. What about my needs, and Claudia's. We love one another, Nonna. We just want to be ordinary people. I'll take her to Australia," he said suddenly, "We'll make a new life there away from all this."

"And do you seriously imagine that you will *have* a life in Australia if you cross Mario? He arranged the contracts for you and your friends. He can just as easily destroy it. Look, Toni, let's go to bed and sleep on it.You don't have to make a decision now. I've lived for forty years with the hope that one day Mario Agusta would pay for what he did. I will never forgive him.Every day I've lived a living death without my Antonio."

What Price Ambition?

"Nonna, that's not true. You've always been there for me and the others. You've always been a lot of fun. Why can't you count your blessings and stop living in the past? If you had really wanted to avenge Antonio's death, you would have done it at the time, and not waited till now. You had three other children with Mario. You shared his bed willingly, Nonna, You couldn't have hated him that much. Maybe he was the one God intended for you all along."
"How dare you! You know nothing, Antonio."
Antonio was not put off.
"And what about his daughter? What about my father's sister? Where does she come into all this?"
Anna sighed and relaxed again.
"Under Italian law she can't inherit, unless there are no male descendants. She had a small inheritance under the will, a villa I think and money. To be honest, I've never made any effort to find out about her. I couldn't make any of this known to her, and I know that Antonio's sister would never say anything. She was terrified of Mario."
"What was his name anyway? Just so that I know where I'm coming from." he added sarcastically.
"The family name is Andresi. Your great-Grandfather was Count Alberto Andresi."
"Count!" said Antonio, and he laughed cynically and shook his head, "This gets more weird by the minute. My father is an Italian nobleman."

What Price Ambition?

He stood up end looked at his Grandmother stonily.
You're right, Nonna. It seems that I know nothing at all.
I just can't get my head round it. Leave me out of your
schemes, Nonna. I'm going to bed."
Anna did not stop him and went to her own room with a
sigh when he disappeared.
However, Antonio did not go to bed right away. His
mind was in a turmoil. It was all just too unreal. He had
grown up with the belief that he was an Agusta, the
branch of the Cosa Nostra which controlled their part of
the City. He had known too that this included some
unsavoury activities, but he had never really given it
much thought. That was something which never
touched his life.
Mario had been just Grandpa to him, and Antonio had
loved him. He still loved him. He realised now that an
accident of birth could never change the closeness he
felt for the man whom he had always known as his
Grandfather. He could not believe that Mario would
ever do him any harm. Mario's motives for killing
Beccy were understandable, if that was what he had
done. He was trying to protect him, Antonio, and he
would not have taken the decision lightly. In spite of
what his Grandmother had said, Antonio did not feel
that Maria was as ruthless as she made out.
Mario was Don. He had to be tough, even ruthless. It
was expected and necessary. Antonio remembered
several times in his life when there had been some

What Price Ambition?

incident or other which had been attributed to Mario.
The boys at school had talked about it in whispers.
Mario was said to have administered justice in a manner
no-one could ignore or forget. Yes, perhaps Mario was
ruthless, but that was the way of it for the Don.
It would be his way too, and Antonio's heart beat faster
at the thought. He was not sure if he could handle it,
and there was only one course of action he could take.
He found that daunting, for it involved confronting
Mario.
He went to bed with images of Mario, the terrible,
towering over him, and bending him to follow the
family code against his will. He was trying to speak to
Mario but every time he tried to say something, the
words came out in an unintelligible garble.
However, in the morning his father rang before he had a
chance to speak to Mario.
"Dad!" exclaimed Antonio in surprise, rubbing the
sleep from his eyes, "What's wrong?"
Giorgio laughed, "Nothing, son. It's good news.
Grandpa asked me to phone you and let you know that
you're leaving for Australia tomorrow. Your ticket and
travellers cheques are at the airport."
"What's the rush?"
"No rush, son. There's no point hanging around now
that you've not got your job in London."
"Jesus! Word gets round fast. I'm not ready to go yet,
Dad. I need to see Claudia."

What Price Ambition?

"You'll have time tomorrow. Your flight doesn't leave till the evening. Your Grandfather wants you to stop off at Singapore. He has a job for you. Mitchell will explain it when he takes you to the airport. How's your Nonna?"
"She's fine," said Antonio abruptly, "Dad, what's going on? What job?"
"Mitchell will explain," repeated his father, "It's something your Grandfather thinks you should know about. Have a good trip, son. We'll try and get out in a couple of months to see you."
"Dad!" said Antonio but Giorgio had rang off,
Antonio got out of bed and pulled on his robe. He made some tea and took it through to his Grandmother who was already awake,
"I heard the phone. Is everything alright?"
"I'm going to Australia tomorrow, Nonna.," he said and sat on the edge of the bed, "I'm sorry I was a bit off-hand last night."
Anna smiled, "That's alright, Toni. It's a lot for a young man to take in all at once. You'll make a fine Don one day. That's why Mario chose you. You're right anyway. It's not your fight. I had some romantic idea that you would help a silly old woman to fulfill a promise. I see now that I was wrong to expect it."
"So you don't hate Grandpa after all."
"Oh yes," said Anna in surprise, "I can never forgive him, and one day he will pay, but I have no right to

come between you and Mario. You know, Antonio, you could become the most powerful man in Europe if you claim your birthright. My Antonio's father owned huge estates in Tuscany. They're still being managed profitably. That and the authority Mario will give you, will mean you will have all the power you need. You haven't forgotten your ambitions, have you?"

"No," said Antonio thoughtfully, "One thing's bothering me, Nonna. If Dad's sister doesn't know about him, how come she's not inherited the estates?"

Anna smiled,- "The lawyers know, and there's Antonio's sister. As I said, she knew. We were good friends, Francesca and I. The girl was just told that she did not inherit. That it was going to another male relative. She was quite young at the time."

"Nonna, do you mind if I take you to the airport this morning. I want to spend some time with Claudia before I go, and I've got things to do."

Anna reached out and touched his cheek,

"Of course not, Antonio," she said fondly, "You go and book my seat and I'll get ready."

Antonio did as she asked and then phoned Claudia. It was still early and Mrs. Ferolla had to get Claudia out of bed.

"Antonio!" she said breathlessly when she came to the phone, "What's wrong?"

Antonio told her he was leaving for Australia next day, and he repeated her name when she did not answer.

What Price Ambition?

When she did, she exploded in a torrent of angry words. "I really hate you, Antonio Agusta. How could you do this to me? You obviously don't love me or you would want to spend some time with me before you leave."
Antonio tried to interrupt her several times, but each time she just raved on at him.
"Claudia, shut up and listen!" he said at last in exasperation.
Claudia stopped abruptly.
"Take tomorrow off work. That's why I'm phoning. I *do* want to spend some time with you. It's not my decision to go early, Claudia. My Grandfather pays the piper and calls the tune, I've got things to do today but be ready at eleven tomorrow. I'll pick you up."
"Yes, Antonio," said Claudia meekly, "I'm sorry. I love you."
Antonio smiled at the change in her tone.
"I love you too, Sweetheart. I'll see you tomorrow."
He dropped his Grandmother off at the airport later that morning and then spent the rest of the day organising his trip, and settling all his bills.
Next morning, he drove to the Ferolla estate where Claudia was waiting impatiently for him. She threw her arms around his neck and kissed him.
"I'm sorry. Let's not waste any more time arguing. You'll be gone soon. I'm coming to the airport with you. Dad's going to pick me up there."

What Price Ambition?

Antonio did not argue. It would mean he could see more of her anyway.

"Come on then. I've got a call to make on the way to lunch."

"Where are we going?" said Claudia, "I'm not dressed for anything up market."

Antonio laughed, "You're fine. We're going on a picnic."

"In January!" exclaimed Claudia.

"Any time, any place," grinned Antonio, "No, I'm not telling you," he added as Claudia started to question him.

Antonio had arranged to pick up a hamper at a delicatessen near his flat, and he opened the wine while Claudia laid out the food on his dining room table.

"To us," he said as he handed her the glass, "I'm going to miss you, Sweetheart."

Claudia lowered her eyelids coyly.

"How much?" she said softly.

"What sort of question is that?" replied Antonio, "More than I've missed anyone before."

He held the chair for Claudia and sat down opposite her.

"Will you miss me enough to take me with you?" Claudia said suddenly, "Oh please, Antonio, let me come with you."

"I can't Sweetheart. You would be too much of a distraction. I've got to concentrate on this project.

What Price Ambition?

Grandpa has invested a lot of money in me and my idea. Besides, we wouldn't have time to get married."
Claudia got up and pulled Antonio's arm.
"Come with me," she said, and crossed to the bedroom. Antonio stopped at the door.
"Claudia, what are you doing?" he said as she started to unbutton her blouse.
"Make love to me, Antonio," she said, and he heard her voice like the beating of his heart. Even the thought made Antonio shiver with excitement, and he felt his body, grow hot with desire. Claudia pulled him towards her, and he drew in his breath sharply when her hands kindled his body into a knife-edge of readiness. She kissed him and he was lost in her arms, his mouth on hers and his thighs pressing the inner softness of her leg. He could not help himself.
He pushed his hand inside her blouse, and felt her breast, soft and heaving with desire. The hardness of her nipples was almost to much for him, and he lifted her off her feet, and carried her to his bed.
Claudia slid the blouse from her shoulders and pulled at his shirt. He pressed closer as her breath became hot and rapid on his face, and he slid his hand under the skirt she wore, until he felt her skin under the lace of her underwear, Claudia gasped when his fingers reached her flesh, and Antonio felt her fumble quickly to pull off the skirt. He helped her with the knickers, and she was naked in his bed. He showered her with

What Price Ambition?

kisses and explored the roundness and softness of her body, lingering playfully around her navel. She held his head with both hands and Antonio felt her arch her body to meet him.
"Oh Antonio," she whispered, "I want you so. I love you."
He squeezed her against him and frantically removed his own clothes, moaning with pleasure when her body touched his. Claudia's hands were like hot coals on his skin as she slid them to his groin and he felt his body grow hard when her fingers caressed him gently.
She buried her face in his neck, and whispered in embarrassment into his ear.
"I didn't know it would be like that. It's throbbing. I'm so excited, Antonio. Teach me to love you," she panted.
She grasped his buttocks with her fingers and slid under him, pushing up towards him with demanding passion. Her legs squeezed against his thighs, and she pulled him close. One thrust and he was into the moistness of her body, enveloping him and inviting him to join with her in a union of wild and complete abandon.
He whispered her name as he pushed into her, and gave himself completely to the rhythm of the need he felt for carnal satisfaction, In a few minutes, he thrust against her, the climax of his desire forcing him into a rigid spasm of ecstasy in the fulfillment of his needs with Claudia, and she stifled a cry as he collapsed on her.

What Price Ambition?

"Claudia, that was magic," he said, and kissed her, "I love you, Sweetheart, It's never been like that with anyone else."
He moved inside her, and he felt her closeness stimulate him again. He made love to her a second time and his head swam with the euphoria of his passion.
So much that he did not notice that Claudia was clinging to him till he relaxed against her.
Her head was buried in his neck, and he felt her shake.
"Claudia, what is it?" he said and raised himself on one elbow, "Didn't you enjoy it, Sweetheart?"
"Oh Antonio," she said and her voice caught in her throat, "I thought it would be the most wonderful experience in my life." she said miserably,
"And it wasn't?" said Antonio incredulously, not believing that she had not felt as he did, "I'm sorry, Sweetheart. It was wonderful for me. I'm really sorry you didn't enjoy it. Was it my fault?"
Claudia clung to him, "I don't know. I don't know what I'm supposed to feel. It was wonderful to begin with. I just thought... no of course it wasn't your fault. I'm just a silly little girl when it comes to sex." she said shyly.
"You're beautiful and you're mine. You'll always be mine now. We'll learn together, Sweetheart. I've always been with girls who have had some experience, you know," he added in embarrassment, for he did not want to talk about anyone else while he lay in Claudia's arms. It was their moment.

What Price Ambition?

Claudia kissed him, "Show me, Antonio. I don't know how to please you."

"Just be you, Sweetheart. You more than please me, and I'm sorry I didn't match that for you. Will you forgive me for being a clumsy idiot? I should have been gentle, should have understood."

"No please don't say that. It just wasn't what I expected that's all. It hurt, but before, before you actually did it, it was nice. I wanted you so much. It was a good feeling, Antonio. I'm sure it will all be good soon. Girls have orgasms which blow their mind."

She looked away shyly, "I've read about it,"

Antonio laughed, "Then I'd better learn how to do it. To tell the truth, I've never thought about it before. I was only interested in what women could do for me, but it's different with you, Claudia. I want to make it good for you too,"

Claudia threw her arms round his neck and kissed him. "You will," she said with a smile, "We'll just have to keep practicing."

"I like it," laughed Antonio, and she giggled when he grabbed her and threw her down on the pillow, "Now seems a good time."

He made love to her again till they both lay exhausted and happy in his bed.

"I didn't want that to happen," said Antonio after a few minutes, "I never wanted to make love to you till we were married."

What Price Ambition?

Claudia moved towards him and put her arms across his chest.

"We are married. You're my husband now. A silly little certificate isn't going to make any difference to the way I feel."

"I don't think your father would see it that way. He won't like it."

"He's not getting It." said Claudia brazenly, and Antonio laughed.

"You know what I mean. You're supposed to be a virgin when we get married."

"No-one is these days. Maybe my mother wasn't either, I don't know. We don't talk about things like that."

"No, I don't suppose mothers do. I know my Grandmother wasn't when she married Grandpa."

Claudia raised herself on one elbow, "You know *that* How?"

"She told me. She had a lover. Can you keep a secret?" Claudia nodded, intrigued by the gossip Antonio was about to tell her.

"Her lover was my real Grandfather. She was pregnant when she married Mario Agusta."

"Antonio!" exclaimed Claudia, "Did your Grandmother really tell you that?"

"Of course she did," said Antonio indignantly, "It isn't something I would make up. What do you take me for?"

"I'm sorry. I'm just surprised, that's all. Your Grandmother! I would never have thought it."

What Price Ambition?

"Well don't you tell anyone, do you hear. I think Mario would flip his lid if he knew."
"Have you met him? Your real Grandfather, I mean."
"No, he's dead. He was killed before my father was born, before Nonna married Mario."
He did not tell Claudia the rest.
"It's still very exciting, Antonio. A whole family you knew nothing about. My mother came from some aristocratic Italian family." she added.
"That's a coincidence..."
Antonio stopped and Claudia looked at him.
"What is?"
With only a slight hesitation, Antonio laughed.
"Nothing. You look like a princess." he said and kissed her.
She threw her arms round his neck and showered him with kisses.
"Hey, do you want to make me miss my plane?"
"Yes," she said honestly, "I don't want you to go."
"I'll be back before you know it. You can come and see me."
Claudia clung to him, "Oh Antonio, I'm going to miss you so."
Antonio was about to agree with her sentiment, but he checked himself when an intrusive foreign thought flashed into his mind.
He would not miss Claudia to the point of distraction. He loved her. At least he thought he did, but now that

he had made love to her it was different. He still loved her, and he wanted to be with her, but he knew that he could enjoy someone else's company if she was not there.

He pushed her gently away, deliberately slowly, trying to rationalise his thoughts.

"Come on. I haven't finished packing yet. Let's get dressed and you can help me."

He jumped off the bed, and went into the bathroom where he turned on the shower.

"There's some new shirts on the table, would you pack them for me, Sweetheart." he called over his shoulder as Claudia started to follow him.

He did not want her with him at that moment, for he needed time to think. It was as if he had only wanted to sleep with her, but he had not felt like that before today. He had meant it when he had told her he loved her, and he wanted her to be his wife. That had not changed. What *had* changed was the way he felt now. His love was no less, his intentions were still the same, but his commitment to Claudia as the single love in his life seemed to have disappeared with her virginity. He did not know what to do about it, so he did nothing. Maybe his love would be reinforced when he was at the other side of the world and missing her.

Claudia did not suspect anything as she said a tearful goodbye, and Antonio boarded the plane with a feeling of guilt hanging over him like a wet blanket.

What Price Ambition?

He shivered involuntarily, like someone was walking over his grave, Nonna would have said. Maybe that was true in a way. Antonio was his real Grandfather's name. Maybe he was trying to say something from the grave. Antonio shrugged it off. He was going to a different world, a new life, and for a while, Claudia would not be part of it. That would surely prove whether or not he loved her.

Chapter 9.

The New World.

As the plane took off into his future, Antonio sighed and looked at the package he was holding, His Grandfather's man, Mitchell, had given it to him when he left him at the airport with instructions for Antonio to open it when he was alone. He had never felt as alone as he did at that moment and he smiled as he opened the envelope.

There was a short fax from his Grandfather with the name and telephone number of a man he was to contact in Singapore. There was also a photograph of a young woman, and Antonio stared at her Malaysian features. "Remember her face," his Grandfather said in his fax, "You'll need to recognize her."

Antonio shifted his eyes back to the photograph. He was not likely to forget her face. She was beautiful, but the most striking thing about her was her blue eyes. They seemed odd in an otherwise oriental face.

The last sentence told him to memorise the detail and destroy everything.

What Price Ambition?

Antonio spent a few a minutes ensuring that it was firmly implanted in his memory, and then he got up and went to the toilet, where he tore up the package and flushed every bit down the pan. Having done that, he returned to his seat and got quietly drunk till he fell asleep.
When he arrived in Singapore, he called the number he had been given as soon as he reached his hotel, and a man called Ron Black answered. Antonio arranged to see him that evening at the hotel and went to bed. He had a feint headache gnawing inside his skull, and he wanted to sleep it off.
However, he had only just got into bed when there was a knock at his door. He sighed and got out again, pulling on his robe. He did not know anyone in Singapore, and he had already dealt with Black. He wrenched open the door impatiently, but stopped abruptly with it half open, for there, in the corridor, was the girl in the photograph.
"Mr. Agusta," she said with a wide smile, "Welcome to Singapore."
Antonio just stared.
"It *is* Antonio Agusta?" she said with a note of uncertainty in her voice.
Antonio recovered from the surprise of seeing her standing there.
"Yes, yes it is, but how did you know? I mean, who are you?"

What Price Ambition?

He almost stuttered in confusion, for her blue eyes disturbed him.
"May I come in?"
Antonio stepped aside to allow her to pass.
He pulled the robe tighter round him and offered her a seat, feeling somewhat vulnerable and embarrassed in her presence.
"Okay, you know my name. So, who are you?"
This time, he had regained his composure, and his tone was business-like.
"I'm Julie Li Chang," she said and smiled again, "My father works for Mario Agusta. He runs the Malaysian business for your Grandfather. Don Mario advised our office that you were coming, and asked us to give you every assistance. So, is there anything I can do for you?"
Antonio's mind immediately focused on what she could definitely do for him personally, and he felt a rush of desire stir in his body beneath the robe.
"You can show me the sights." he said as calmly as he could, while his pulse quickened at the secret thoughts in his head.
Julie Li Chang laughed, a light, high-pitched sound like water falling over rocks.
"Most men are more personal. You don't fancy me, Mr. Agusta?"

What Price Ambition?

Antonio looked boldly at her without smiling. He did not like her direct approach. It was not his style, and it made him feel vulnerable and inadequate.
"Yes, I'll screw you if you'll let me," he said brazenly, "But I'm not bothered one way or the other."
He saw her cheekbones turn a delicate shade of rose under the coffee coloured skin, and her eyes flickered for a second.
"I'm sorry if I offended you, Mr. Agusta. Men usually get the wrong idea, so I make it clear right at the start that I'm not for hire. This is business, no more no less."
Antonio nodded, "Sure. Suits me." but his heart pounded at the thought of the chase. She had made the mistake of declaring herself, and now he just had to have her.
"Fine. Then I'll see you in the bar at nine. We can go somewhere."
"No, not tonight," said Antonio quickly for he did not know how long his meeting with Ron Black would take, "I'll meet you for breakfast tomorrow."
She offered him her hand as she stood up to leave, and Antonio shook it firmly, dropping touch.
He stared at the closed door when she had gone, and almost jumped when an image of Claudia seemed to appear from out of the paintwork. This was what he had felt back at his flat. Claudia in one little private niche of his life, while he felt an attraction for another women. He did not even feel guilty. Claudia would never know.

What Price Ambition?

He could live in both worlds. Claudia as his wife and mother of his children and yet still satisfy his desires wherever the fancy took him. It did not mean he loved Claudia any less. At least, that was how he rationalised it, but still he had an uneasy feeling.

He met Ron Black in the hotel bar, and they found a quiet corner.

"You've seen the photograph?" Ron asked without beating about the bush.

Antonio smiled, "Yes, very tasty, *and* I've met her." His eyes were alight with the memory.

Ron Black's eyes narrowed, "She's contacted you already?"

"Yes, last night, just after I arrived. Why?"

"What did she want?"

"Just to introduce herself, and see if I needed anything. Look, what is this?"

Ron Black leaned forward, "Her old man is staging a coup against the Don. He has been talking to one of the Triad groups out here. They plan to take over the Malaysian operation for themselves."

Antonio frowned, "But I thought the Triads had this area pretty sewn up anyway. What's Grandpa involved in out here?"

Ron Black leaned even closer, "He didn't tell you?"

Antonio shook his head, "No, he said I would be briefed out here."

What Price Ambition?

"Okay. Your Grandfather runs cigarettes into China and other cargo out. The Triads want his logistics operation."

"This other cargo, it wouldn't be drugs, would it?"

"What do you think? That's where the money is."

"Fuck him!" said Antonio softly, "Look, I'm not sure I want to be part of this."

Ron Black looked at him with astonishment.

"Sorry?" he said incredulously, "I thought that the Don had named you as his successor."

"Yes, he has, but I didn't realise just what I was getting into."

Black laughed cynically, "Come off it, Agusta, you would have to be fucking naive not to have some idea of what's going on."

"I'm beginning to realise it," said Antonio grimly.

"How does Julie Li Chang fit into this?" he added, changing the subject

"They're using her to open up new routes out. You saw how much of a looker she is. Well, she's using her obvious charms to get to influential businessmen and persuade them to let her father export goods out of Malaysia. It's all legitimate of course and it turns a good profit, but the shipments also include the dope. She's supposed to persuade you to go over to their side."

Antonio smiled and thought of Julie. Her attitude must have been deliberately distant to attract him.

What Price Ambition?

"Well it worked," he said out loud, "I was planning to screw her, but forearmed is forewarned. I'm going to enjoy this."

"Watch your back," said Ron shortly, "Her father is a powerful man, and she's a clever lady, The Don wants you to find out what she's up to and then axe her."

"Axe her?" said Antonio puzzled.

"Get rid of her, kill her, whatever. He wants to warn her father not to cross him." said Black without feeling."

"No, I'm not into murder. I'll see what I can find out, but the girl is not to be harmed."

Black shrugged, "Have it your own way. I'm only telling you our orders."

Antonio stood up, "I don't take orders from anyone," Black looked up at him with a slight smile on his lips, "You're an Agusta aren't you?" he said simply and laughed.

"That doesn't make me a moronic puppet," said Antonio angrily and he saw Black's eyes narrow. Antonio tensed, but Black did not move.

"Like I said, it's your funeral, Mr. Augusta."

Antonio nodded and turned to leave, but he stopped at Black's shoulder.

"There's more ways than one to peel an orange. Maybe she'll come over to us."

"You can try, but I thought you were already engaged to the Ferolla girl."

What Price Ambition?

"I am, but I'm not talking about marriage here. Singapore is a long way from London."
Black laughed, "Boy, have you got some learning to do about women. They can smell another woman at the end of the phone. Then you'll be in the shit. Dimitri Ferolla isn't known for his sunny, placid nature."
"Let me worry about that."
"I intend t. I don't want any part of it. Well maybe I'd let her share my bed," he laughed, "I'd just top her when you've got what you want."
"You're not me," said Antonio softly, "Don't worry so much, Ron. I won't let you down."
Antonio walked away, his shoulders square, and his stride confident.
"I hope not, son," said Black under his breath.
Antonio went back to his room to phone Claudia but he had forgotten that it was only the afternoon there, and she was still at work, so he went to bed.
He met Julie for breakfast next morning, and they shared a pleasant meal.
"So, you have a business degree, and an important job in your father's organisation. Do you find time for a social life too?"
Julie smiled, "Oh yes, I have to socialise as part of my duties, and my mother is dead so my father needs a hostess for his entertaining,"

What Price Ambition?

"I meant on a personal basis. Do you have a boyfriend?"

Julie smiled again, "No, Mr. Agusta, I don't have any personal involvement with anyone right now. I'm too busy."

Antonio shifted his gaze from the coffee he was stirring to her face, and Julie looked away shyly.

"You asked me a question," he said slowly, "And I think that gives me the right to ask you the same question." he smiled slightly, "Do you fancy me, Julie?"

She hesitated and her eyes flickered, but she continued to look him in the eye.

"I find you a very attractive man, Mr. Agusta." she said softly.

"Then it shouldn't be difficult for us to become more personally involved. I fancy you. You fancy me. We're an item."

"Not quite. I might fancy you, but I'm not stupid, Mr. Agusta, and neither are you. I think we're both playing this game at our father's bidding. You want information from me, and I want to win your trust enough to convert you to our way of thinking."

Antonio smiled, "My Grandfather," he corrected, "Mario is my Grandfather. Look, why don't we forget them for today. I'd like you to show me the sights. No strings attached. If you want to walk away at the end of the day, no problem, and if we find that we're

What Price Ambition?

irresistibly attracted, I'd like to sleep with you tonight. Deal?"
Julie smiled, "Deal. That's certainly the most succinct and interesting proposition I've had for some time. Nice doing business with you, Antonio."
Antonio did sleep with Julie that night, or for the next two nights. On the third, they lay in bed together with Julie's head resting against Antonio's shoulder.
"It's time to discuss business, Antonio," she whispered without looking at him, "The party's over. I need to know where you stand."
Antonio sighed, "Yes, I suppose you're right. I had a phone call from Grandpa this afternoon, He wants results. Damn them! Damn them all."
Julie lifted her head.
"You don't mean that. Hasn't it always been your destiny to take over form your Grandfather, just as mine is to marry the man my father has chosen for me."
"You're going to be married," said Antonio in surprise, "Then, why?" he stopped without forming the question.
Julie laughed, "My marriage has been arranged since I was a child. "He is not an attractive man. I take what I want now, for this time next year, my duty will be to my husband."
"You're a strange one."
Julie smiled, "No more so than you, Antonio. You're going to marry Claudia Ferolla. Your Grandfather has signed a contract, yet here you are in my bed. Not the

actions of a man who professes to be in love with his fiancée."

Antonio laughed, "Okay, so we're soul mates. What now? I'm in the Agusta corner. Where do you and your father stand, Julie?"

She sat up and Antonio looked at her olive-coloured body, sinewy and slender, even verging on thin. She was beautiful, like one of the golden idols he had seen in the temples. She made love with him beautifully too, but her passion was as if it had been orchestrated by centuries of subservience, He could not fault her explicit sexual knowledge, and her ability to excite him beyond reason, but she did not have the vibrant basic needs Claudia had shown in her Latin abandon with him. Nor could she compare with the feeling of deep love Claudia stirred in him, and for a minute, he felt guilty. However, it soon disappeared when Julie spoke.

"Your Grandfather is out of touch with the market demands in the East. We need to move in while everything is in chaos. We need to move now, but Don Agusta won't see it. My father wants to break away from the Agusta empire and set up his own Eastern network.

"With the Triads?"

"If that's what it takes."

"Well at least you're honest, Julie and I'm grateful for that.

What Price Ambition?

I'll try and be mutually forthcoming. I've got the information I was told to find out. You've just given it to me. Now I have to stop your father. How can I do that, Julie?"

He looked directly at her without any sign of emotion in his eyes.

"You can't Antonio," said Julie with a frown, "The deal is done, and besides, there's a third party involved. No, I won't tell you."

She held up her hands to silence his question before he asked it, but she hesitated and Antonio saw the dilemma in her eyes, "I *will* tell you that you should look at the shadows around you. All is not as it seems on the face of it. No more. I've said too much already."

She held up her hands again.

"Someone else said something similar recently," said Antonio, "I'm beginning to think I'm in a snake pit with no way out except to slay all the snakes and make myself a ladder with the skins."

His eyes narrowed and he looked at her keenly.

"If your father is determined to go ahead, he's declared war on the Agusta family. You know I'll have to stop him. We can't let him take any of it."

"Yes, I know and that's why I was hoping you would see it differently. It's an opportunity, Antonio. We know the East much better than you. We don't want to take anything which belongs to Don Agusta, but we do want to seize all the business which is out there. Don Agusta is of the old school, and I thought you would be more progressive."

"I'm not entirely a closed book. Run it past me, and let's see if I can jump aboard without catching my coat tail in the door. What's in it for me?"

Julie smiled, "I said it was nice doing business with you. "You can have the European distribution network, just as we have it here for your Grandfather in Malaysia."

"And what do you want from me?"

Julie did not hesitate, "We want you to tell Don Agusta that his business here is dead. Persuade him that he no longer has a future in the Far East. He can buy his drugs from any source, probably cheaper than he can find and ship his own supplies. Tell him not to interfere, Antonio. It's a dangerous business."

That sounds like a threat, Julie."

Julie shrugged, "It's a fact, Antonio. I said the deal is done. If we have to, we'll fight you for the right to operate independently, but I hope you will see the logic of it and persuade him to withdraw quietly. My father is prepared to pay compensation for loss of business over a transitional period, say two years. We will supply half your stock free for that period."

Antonio whistled, "Generous but I don't know if Grandpa will go for it. He doesn't like his boat to be rocked."

What Price Ambition?

Then persuade him, Antonio. It's a good business deal for him. He won't have any of the headaches that go with the territory."
"You'll have to leave it with me for a couple of days. I need to speak to Grandpa, and it will probably take several calls before he calms down enough to listen."
Julie agreed and snuggled up to him again.
"One for the road," she whispered softly, and Antonio felt the closeness of her body stimulate his desire once more.
It was late when he left Julie's apartment, but he called Ron Black anyway.
"We need to meet." said Antonio shortly,
"Sure, but can't it wait till morning. I've got other business tonight."
Antonio heard a female giggle in the background and he laughed.
"Sure, I can hear that. Okay, have fun. I'll see you first thing."
"Well, you've got the run-down on their operation. Well done, Mr. Agusta. I didn't rate your chances much. I underestimated you," said Ron Black with a grudging smile.
"I learned more than that. I sure have been naive, and I still don't know that I want any part of the drugs business. It honestly never occurred to me that Grandpa was into that. I'm not sure what I should do."

What Price Ambition?

Antonio was not sure about taking Ron Black into his confidence. He had only just met the man but still there was something about him he could respect.
"That depends on whether you're still with us all the way, or maybe you were tempted by the offer she made."
"And what do you think?"
"I hope you're still an Agusta. It would surely complicate things if you weren't."
Antonio smiled, "You're a good Family man, Ron. Of course I'm for Mario. He's my Grandfather."
Suddenly, Anna's words came back to him. Mario was not his Grandfather. He dismissed it quickly. Mario was the man he had been brought up to love and admire, and to all intents and purposes, he was his Grandfather.
"I was only testing the water to see how far they would go," he went on, "I've no intention of taking up their offer unless Grandpa wants to go ahead and let them run their own operation."
Black shook his head, "No way. My instructions are to stop them, whatever they're up to and whatever it takes, but speak to the Don. Maybe he'll see it differently if you put it to him. You can phone him now. It's only about eleven back home."
Antonio went to his room and phoned his Grandfather. He was not surprised when Mario thundered his refusal down the phone.

What Price Ambition?

"No, no, no, Antonio!" he shouted, "There can be no deal. He's stolen from the Family. He will stop now or we'll stop him."

"Ling won't stop, Grandpa," said Antonio, when Mario had finished ranting.

"Then you must make him stop. Ron Black will know how."

"Okay, Grandpa. I'll do what you want. Ling will cease to trade, one way or the other."

Antonio said it half-heartedly, for he knew it was going to be unpleasant.

Ron Black, however, did not see any problem.

"You have two options. You eliminate Ling himself, or you put pressure on him by teaching him a little lesson. I personally would go for the second option."

Antonio raised his eyebrow in an unspoken question and Black went on.

"If you teach him a lesson he won't forget, and make it highly visible, no-one will try it on again with the Agusta Family."

"How?"

"Kill the girl. He thinks she's the sun and moon. Kill her and he'll be a broken man. He won't have any fight left in him."

Antonio put his fingers together and tapped his lips, his elbows on the arms of the chair to stop the twitching he felt building up. He considered what Black had said for some time without speaking. The whole idea sickened him to the stomach, but around the edges of his conscience he heard a little voice telling him that Black was talking sense. It was a different world from the one he thought he had been brought up in. Now he was seeing the ruthless Mario whom his Grandmother spoke of.

"Okay," he said finally, "But I don't want to do it."

"Of course not. We have button men whose job it is to handle this. You just get her where they can take her without any hassle. Take her for a drive. I'll give you the route."

Ron Black left Antonio alone and he walked out into the garden to the side of the pool. He could not believe he had just given his consent and approval for someone to be killed, not just someone, but a girl he had slept with last night. He liked Julie. He did not want her hurt, let alone killed, and his mind was in turmoil. Something was happening to him, inside, in his heart, in his head where he had no control. It was as if he was standing on the sideline, and watching someone else step into Mario's shoes. Someone who was like Mario, who accepted the way of the Family without question or compromise. He was not sure if he would be able to go through with it.

He walked for nearly two hours round the gardens, and then out into the thronging streets of Singapore. He sat in a bar for another two or three hours, and then returned to the hotel and lay on his bed.

What Price Ambition?

When Julie rang for him, she was given a message Antonio had left, telling her that he had had to go out for the evening, but that he would pick her up at her apartment next morning early.

It was coming up to six when Antonio climbed out of the fire escape in the hotel and drove to the street where Julie lived. He had hired a car using another name and a false passport provided by Black, and he checked the street before he got out to make sure it was empty. He wore a woollen hat pulled low over his head, and a chain store denim jacket. It was chilly in the early morning mist, and he did not look out of place.

Julie was ready and he greeted her fondly. She suspected nothing as he took her arm, and guided her quickly to the car. No-one was about in the fashionable district where she lived, and they left the city for the hills beyond.

By the time they reached the tree-line, the sun was strong.

"Let's stop, Antonio," said Julie, "It's so hot. We could sit in the shade of the trees for a while."

"Just a couple more miles," said Antonio, purposely avoiding eye contact with her. He did not want to see the trust and friendship there, or let her see the sorrow in his eyes.

The spot Black had chosen was particularly picturesque, and Julie got out of the car as soon as it stopped, and walked to a small clearing where some picnic benches had been erected. Antonio hesitated and let her go forward alone.

"Come on, Antonio," she laughed, and turned back towards him.

The two men ran silently from the trees, and grabbed Julie before she knew what was happening. One of them raised his hand to deliver a lethal blow to her neck, but she was struggling so much that he missed and hit her shoulder.

Julie sank to the ground, her arm paralysed by the attack, and she screamed.

The other man kicked out at her and caught her in the side of the face. Blood gushed from the wound which split her cheek.

"Stop it!" cried Antonio in horror, "Not like this."

"The bitch is struggling too much" said one man, "She nearly, had my hand off there." he added nursing his hand which Julie had bitten furiously in her struggle for life.

"Okay, let's finish her off," said the other man, and drew out a wicked looking knife which glinted in the sun. In seconds he had thrust it into Julie's chest and twisted upwards to her heart. Julie seemed to pause in mid air, and with her hands held out to Antonio she pleaded with her eyes for help.

"Why?" she whispered as blood trickled from the corners of her mouth.

What Price Ambition?

She stumbled forward, and collapsed at Antonio's feet, face down in the grass.
Antonio froze and looked curiously at the blood stains and thought momentarily in a detached sort of way, how strange it was that the stain seeping into the grass was brown.
The man who had stabbed Julie, bent down and roughly pulled her head to the side, and Antonio stepped back with a start, Julie's eyes stared at him accusingly.
"She's dead." the man said shortly.
Antonio turned away, and held his stomach. He wanted to be sick, but even the miserable feeling of nausea could not induce the retching to relieve his feeling of horror. He stumbled towards a bench, and sat down heavily, breathing deeply to regain his composure.
"We're to take her to her father's house and dump her on the doorstep," said the other man, looking at Antonio with disdain, "You'd better get back to the hotel. Your breakfast will be delivered in an hour."
Antonio raised his hand and nodded. He could not look at Julie's body. It was bad enough that her accusing eyes were haunting him.
Antonio was in a daze as he drove back to the City, and left the car at the hire office.
The hotel was quite busy, and he waited his chance to slip in with a group of tourists who had just arrived.
With a few minutes to spare after he had undressed and got into bed, his breakfast arrived.

What Price Ambition?

The sight of the food made him retch, and he poured himself a brandy with the coffee. He was expecting Black to ring, and on cue, the shrill noise of the bell jangled his already shot nerves.

"Okay, " said Black, "It's done. Ling has got the message. Now you reinforce it."

Antonio's finger shook as he pressed the buttons to dial Julie's father's number. His voice sounded high-pitched and strangulated when he spoke at first, but in a second, he was composed.

"I think you got our message, Mr. Ling. Back off now, or it's your son's turn next. I believe he has two children too."

"What sort of man are you?" shouted Ling, "You're an animal, Agusta. Julie could do you no harm."

"You said it, Ling, and I'm a real sadist when I want. They don't have to die immediately."

Ling strangled a sob, "You will be punished by your ancestors, young man," he said quietly, "Very well, I have no choice. I will retire as the Agusta agent, and stop all negotiation with the Triads. I will hand over to someone of your choosing. You didn't have to kill her."

Antonio felt the guilt Ling wanted him to feel and more. "What about this third party?" Antonio said brusquely, "Who is it?"

Ling laughed harshly, "You'll find out, Mr. Agusta. They won't like this at all." and the phone went dead.

What Price Ambition?

Ling's wards rang in Antonio's ears, as he redialled and called his Grandfather.
"Sorry,. Grandpa," he said wearily, when Mario had to get out of bed to speak to him, "Ling has capitulated. He won't bother us any more, but he said something strange, Grandpa. Did you know he has a partner?"
"No, I didn't," said Mario in surprise, "Do you know who it is, Antonio?"
"No, but I have a feeling it's someone we know. Julie..." Antonio's voice faltered for a second, "Ling's daughter hinted as much."
"You've done well, Antonio. Leave the rest to Black now. You go on to Australia. You've got a whole new life ahead of you there."
"I hope so, Grandpa," said Antonio with a heavy heart, "I don't like this one very much right now. Tell Nonna I love her and I'm missing her."
He put down the phone abruptly before Mario could say anything to him, and suddenly, in a frenzy of self-hate, he ripped off his robe, and ran to the shower where he scrubbed himself till his skin was red and sore. He increased the temperature of the water, but still he felt soiled and unclean. He could not rid himself of the image of Julie's eyes, and even the prospect of achieving the dream he had harboured as a child was no consolation. He was embroiled in another life, an evil, sordid existence of murder, extortion, drugs and money laundering. He held people's lives dangling on a series

What Price Ambition?

of inter-connected strings, like a puppet. At a whim, depending on whatever mood he was in, he could sever any one of them. No-one in the world could cross him and carry on unscathed, for there would always be someone at his shoulder to administer the Family vendetta.
He had never wanted any of it. He had always dismissed it from his mind, not admitting it to himself or to anyone else. None of his friends or even those who did not like him too much would dare raise the subject for fear of reprisals from the Agustas. Not in his mind, not in existence. That was how he had handled it, but now it was here, right with him. There was no escape. He was an Agusta. He was *the* Agusta. Bathing would never be the same again, and it terrified his inner soul.

Chapter 10.

Relatively Speaking.

The sun was hot in Brisbane when Antonio started to descend the steps from the plane, and he blinked in the bright light. The formalities were quick and he passed through the exit to scan the crowds milling around. Someone called his name, and he turned with a smile to meet Drew and Rick who had come to meet him. He hugged them both like brothers, and went with them to the bar before they left the airport.
"You'll have to get used to the cold beer." laughed Drew as Antonio pulled a face.
"Well, guys, how's it going?"
"Couldn't be better, cobber," mimicked Drew in a passable Australian accent.
"They're going to let me have a test run in two months, and married life is great."
"And the job Mr. Morrow gave me in the factory is great too," said Rick, Tool making, and I can make any parts we need. Mr. Morrow says it's okay."

What Price Ambition?

"I hope they're not expecting too much. It's one thing modifying our own car to perform better, but putting the design on paper and building a working model to use on other cars. That's something else."
Drew slapped Antonio's shoulder, "Come on, genius, I never took modesty to be one of your virtues,"
Antonio laughed, "No, I suppose not. How's your wife, Drew?"
"She's fine. It's great. No more nights prowling round the clubs looking for someone willing. How about you, Pal? When are you tying the knot?"
"Not for a while yet. I don't intend to go back to the UK for a few years, and I don't want Claudia out here."
Rick laughed, "Still got the roving eye, Pal."
"Sure," grinned Antonio, "That's something I never intend to give up."
"I thought you were in love with this Italian girl," said Drew.
"Yes, I am. She's some babe."
"Then you shouldn't be running after other women,"
"Listen to the old married man," laughed Rick, "We'll have to drag him away from Monica for a few nights on the town."
Drew's face took on a serious look,"No, it's the real thing for me fellas. I joke about it but I don't want anyone else, and if you really love your girl, Antonio, you won't either."

What Price Ambition?

Antonio drank his beer quickly, for he suddenly felt guilty. The feeling he had thought he would never experience had suddenly taken hold of him, and was devouring his resolve.

"Maybe you're right, Drew. I think I'll give women a miss completely for a while. I'll have enough on my mind anyway."

"Pull the other one, Agusta," said Rick, and he ordered another round for them.

Antonio surprised them. He became totally absorbed in the work in the research and development department in the factory. He learned how to put his ideas on paper with the help of a design engineer and a computer. He was taught about the different materials, and the limits to their use. He worked with Rick and the toolmaker to see how the raw materials could be shaped and turned into what they needed.

Claudia was never far from his thoughts but she was not important in his life right now, and it was with some surprise that he read the letter from his parents. They told him that they would be visiting and would be bringing

Claudia to see him some two months after he had first arrived. He was not sure he wanted the disruption yet, but they had already made their plans and would be arriving in a few days.

Antonio was looking forward to seeing Claudia, but he was not prepared for the instant fire in his gut which hit him when he first saw her. He almost forgot to breathe in his excitement. He did love her, and he wanted her. Claudia blushed as he raised her hand to his lips when they met.

"You're more beautiful than ever," he whispered as he kissed her cheek and her face glowed with pleasure. However, she tossed her black hair and her eyes flashed at him.

"I've missed you, Antonio. Four emails, that's all I've had from you. I thought you loved me."

"I'm sorry, Sweetheart. I'm not much of a letter writer, and I've been working really hard. I'll make it up to you. Of course I love you. It's not been much fun for me either. I missed you too."

At the first opportunity, he left his parents to unpack and rest, and he went back to Claudia's room.

They made love passionately and with deep feeling, and as they lay in bed, he felt Claudia's fingers caress his chest.

"Antonio," she said softly, and he murmured an acknowledgement as he lay and enjoyed the sensation, "I think I might be pregnant."

Antonio sat up so suddenly that he caught Claudia's chin with his elbow and she cried out.

"I'm sorry, Sweetheart. You can't be, Claudia. We only had one day together before I left."

"I'm afraid to go to the doctor. What are we going to do Antonio?"

What Price Ambition?

"I don't know. I don't need this hassle right now." and of course, that was the worst thing he could have said. Claudia started to cry.
"Don't you want to marry me, Antonio?" she sniffed.
Antonio held her in his arms, "Don't cry, Sweetheart. It was a shock right out of the blue like that. Of course I do, but not yet. You understand, Sweetheart, don't you? I need to concentrate on my work, It's important."
That made Claudia cry even more.
"I thought I was important to you too," she sobbed, "What will Dad say? We've never had anyone get pregnant in the family before. Mum will be devastated. She's such a lady. She is a lady, you know. Her Grandfather was Count Alberto Andresi."
Antonio froze, and his heart skipped several beats.
"Are you kidding me? Who was your great Grandfather?"
"I told you, Count Alberto Andresi. His son was killed before he could inherit, They say there was a Grandson too, my mother's half brother, but he has never claimed his inheritance."
Antonio got out of bed, and pulled on his clothes without looking at Claudia.
"What's wrong, Antonio. Are you angry that I'm pregnant?"
She touched his shoulder, but he shrugged her off,

What Price Ambition?

"Yes, no, not angry. I've got to think about this, Claudia," he said abruptly, "I've got to go. I'll see you in the morning."
"Antonio, what's wrong? Please talk to me," Claudia cried.
"I've got to go," repeated Antonio and he kissed her cheek briefly, and left in a hurry.
He had to get out of that room. He could not bear to touch Claudia. She was his cousin. His father and her mother were brother and sister.
"Christ!" he said out loud as he got in his car, and drove to his flat, "She's pregnant!"
He felt sick. He had just got his cousin pregnant, an act which could prove to be disastrous for the baby they would produce. They were too closely related.
"Christ!" he said again, "What have I done?"
Next day he did not answer the phone, and Claudia was in tears when his parents saw her. They too tried in vain to contact him, but he was never available. For the remainder of their holiday, Antonio avoided both Claudia and his mother and father by working late and leaving early. Once, they called at his flat late and managed to see him, but he refused to discuss it with them, and despite his mother's pleas for him to see Claudia, he would not change his mind. He could not bear to look at her in his anguish.
They took Claudia home, a young girl bewildered, physically sick with hurt and worry and pregnancy. She

What Price Ambition?

had hardly eaten anything since Antonio had walked out on her, and was becoming visibly ill.
Antonio was hurting too, and bursting with anger. It was obscene. His Grandmother's indiscretion had caused him to have a union with a girl who was his own flesh and blood. His skin crawled when he thought about Claudia. She was no longer a suitable partner for him, and he could not tell anyone, so he shut out the tender memories of her which kept pushing to the front of his mind. He *had* loved her, loved her dearly, but the horror now filling him was over-riding even that emotional pull. He could not help it. Fate had dealt him a blow, and he could not cope with it. Of all the girls in the world, why did it have to be his? He had no answer to that, and he shut her out of his mind forever. He did not answer the phone to his friends either, and when they called to see if he was alright, he told them to leave him alone. He went to work, though, and worked long hours without taking breaks, or enjoying any leisure pursuits.
Rick and Drew were worried but they could not get through to him, for he seemed to have blocked everything from his life.
After several weeks of not answering calls or seeing anyone, Antonio left the factory late one evening, picked up a take-away meal and went home. He unlocked the door as usual, but when he switched on

What Price Ambition?

the light at the living room door, he stopped with his hand still lingering on the switch.
"Black! What are you doing in my flat?"
"Gooday, Mr, Agusta," said Ron Black, "Your Grandfather is in one hell of a temper. It seems you're not answering your phone, and all hell has broken loose."
"It's nothing to do with me," said Antonio, and got himself a beer from the fridge, "Do you want one?" he added,
"Thanks. You might not think so, but Miss Ferolla says it's got everything to do with you. She told her old man that she's pregnant. That was careless, Mr. Agusta, Don Dimitri is gunning for you."
"She can get an abortion. It's not my fault if the girl is stupid. I only slept with her once."
"But you're engaged. Your Grandfather has signed a contract. What's changed, Antonio?"
Antonio looked away from Ron, for the familiarity he used to address him had weakened his resolve.
"It's none of your business. I've changed my mind, I don't want to marry her and I don't want the kid."
"Well, your Grandfather is ringing you in half an hour, I'm to see you take the call."
Antonio did not say anything, for he knew that Ron would carry out his Grandfather's instruction to the letter.

What Price Ambition?

"Well, if you're staying, you might as well help me eat this Chinese."
They sat down silently to share the meal.
"Don't give me any hassle, Grandpa," said Antonio when he eventually spoke to Mario, "I don't want to marry her. No, I don't care if she is pregnant. How do I know it's mine anyway? I only slept with her once. Look, Grandpa, there is no way I'm ever going to get back with Claudia Ferolla. If you want to know, she makes me sick."
Mario shouted at him, but Antonio was not listening, "I've given my word, Antonio," Mario said, "You'll have to marry her. You can do what you like after the wedding. Live apart, take a mistress, I don't care, but you must honour the contract."
"Get stuffed, Grandpa," shouted Antonio, and slammed the phone down.
It rang again in a few seconds
"It's your Grandmother," said Ron when Antonio made no attempt to pick it up.
"Don't start, Nonna" said Antonio before Anna could say anything.
"I won't start anything, Toni," said Anna softly. What is it? You can tell me. Haven't we always been friends?"
Antonio turned to Ron, "Take a walk, Black. I want to talk to Nonna in private,.

What Price Ambition?

Ron Black left the apartment without any argument, and Antonio returned the phone to his ear.
"You're the only one I *can* talk to, Nonna. God, what a mess!"
Anna waited for him to continue.
"Nonna, did you know that Claudia's mother is an Andresi, She's my father's sister, Nonna."
He heard the sharp intake of breath at the other end of the line.
"Did you hear what I said, Nonna?" Antonio demanded impatiently, "Mrs. Ferolla is your dead lover's daughter. I've been sleeping with my cousin. We have the same Grandfather. Of God, it makes me sick."
"I didn't know, Antonio. Mario only said that Claudia's background was suitable, but of course he has no idea about your father. I'm sorry, but it's maybe not as bad as you make out. It *is* possible for cousins to marry. You can't have changed your feelings for Claudia just like that."
Antonio paused, and when he spoke, his voice was cold, and with a certainty which put dread into Anna's heart
"I've changed my feelings for her completely. I can't marry her. It isn't right. I don't feel it's right. I couldn't even touch her again."
"And what about the baby, Antonio, your baby?"
"She'll have to get rid of it. She can't have it. It could be a monster."

What Price Ambition?

"Don't be silly, Antonio. Of course it won't, and Claudia can have tests if there's any doubt."
"How can she, Nonna?" said Antonio bitterly, "Why would she want to under normal circumstances. She's a normal healthy woman for any other man. I can't tell anyone why I've cooled towards her. No-one knows the truth. You don't want Grandpa to find out, do you?"
Anna did not reply for a few seconds.
"No, I don't," she said at last, "Yes, you're right. Antonio, but this isn't going to be easy for you. Claudia's father was angry, and the poor girl is devastated."
"You'll have to find a way, Nonna. This is your doing. I'm not marrying her and that's final."
A wave of intense sadness gripped his heart as he said the words, and just for a brief moment, he wavered in his intent. He had loved Claudia, and if he was honest with himself, he could not just dismiss his feelings as if he had never known her. However, it was so brief that in another instant he was reiterating his statement to his Grandmother.
"I think you're making too much of denying your feelings for Claudia," said Anna softly, "You can't fool me, Antonio, but I'll do as you want for the time being."
Antonio shut Claudia out of his mind for the rest of the year, refusing to answer even letters. Through his Grandmother, he learned that Claudia had an abortion,

What Price Ambition?

and had gone to live in Italy with her Grandparents to recover.
There was bitter recriminations from the Ferolla Family, but all Anna would tell Mario was that Antonio had realised that he did not love Claudia when they had met in Australia, and to save her feelings he had severed relations
with her there and then.
Mario was furious.
"What sort of reason is that?" he thundered, "Is the boy totally mad? She's not unattractive. He obviously liked her when he slept with her, so what's his problem? What's this love anyway? Marriage is about building a partnership, as we know only too well, Anna. We've been happy together haven't we, woman?"
Anna looked at Mario, but she did not answer him directly
"It was a different world in our day, Mario. Young people these days need emotional stability, as well as the material benefits of a good marriage. They don't marry as a business arrangement any more."
"He was happy enough to agree to it to get what he wanted. An Agusta does not go back on his word."
Anna bit her lip, She wanted to tell Mario that Antonio was not an Agusta, but she was afraid. Even now, the violence smouldered in Mario under the surface.
She had seen first hand what he could do, and she was afraid.

What Price Ambition?

Dimitri Ferolla broke off all relations with the Agusta Family, and although he had not issued a vendetta against Antonio, he made it clear they were enemies. Antonio knew it meant that the Ferollas would take every opportunity to bring him down, and probably go out of their way to achieve it.

Knowing that his future was at the very least uncertain, with even the support of his Grandfather visibly withdrawn, Antonio worked hard and played hard. He earned a reputation in the city as man who knew how to party. He was never short of companions, male and female, but his only friends were Rick and Drew.

Drew finished his first professional race in fifteenth position, and he somersaulted out of the car at the end with a shriek of delight.

"I did it! I did it!" he shouted, and hugged Antonio, "I'm going to be at the front this time next year. Just you wait and see."

"Sure you will," said Antonio enthusiastically, "Next year is going to be the best year ever."

However, the New Year did not start well for Antonio. When his work permit expired, he was refused renewal. When he went to plead his case, the official he saw was adamant, but refused to give any indication why the Australian Government had suffered a change of heart. Ron Black made his own enquiries.

What Price Ambition?

"I'm sorry, Antonio. It seems that Mr. Ferolla has a stronger pull than your Grandfather. They've vetoed your visa. You'll have to leave in a month."

"The bastard! Now what am I going to do?"

He rang his Grandfather, but Mario was non-committal. He was sick of the whole business. It had cost him credibility, and consequently, business, and he felt control was slipping away.

"There's nothing I can do, Antonio. You've built your wall around you, and you'll just have to find a way to knock it down. I wash my hands of it."

Antonio was silent for a second, and Mario had to ask if he was still at the end of the line.

"Yes, I'm here, Grandpa. You're obviously regretting nominating me."

"Yes, if you must know, but *my* word is law. You will inherit from me, but god knows what will be left to give you. You'll have to build your own reputation, and I'm sorry to say you haven't got off to a very good start. I'll do what I can while I can, but it's slipping away, Antonio. Ferolla was behind the Singapore coup. You stopped that, and that's another reason for him to hate you. He's been moving in, and I'm having a job to hold him back without an all- out war between us. I'm sorry you'll have to curb your ambitions in the racing circuit, but you've brought it on yourself."

He paused, "Claudia came to see 'me," he said with a noticeable softening of his tone, "She's really a very

What Price Ambition?

nice girl, but she's so ill. She wanted to tell me she loved you, and still does. She wanted me to know it wasn't her doing to sever relations between our families. She doesn't want you hurt. That's why you're still alive, Antonio. Claudia stopped her father from taking any action.
You haven't been fair to that girl. She doesn't understand why, and I must say, I'm at a loss to understand too."
"I just don't love her any more," said Antonio in his rehearsed speech, but he knew that was not true either. He felt a pang of tenderness clutch his heart every time he thought about Claudia, and he was sorry he had caused her pain. It was not her fault. She did not know the reasons for his change of heart, and he could not tell her, or his Grandfather.
When he had spoken to Mario, he went out to a bar, intending to get drunk, but he could not even do that. After a few drinks on his own, he left the smoky atmosphere, and drove out of the city to the hills where the air was clear.
It was a warm night as always in Australia, and he sat on a rock looking across the valley in the moonlight, the red glow of the landscape giving it an eerie lunar appearance in the blue light from the moon.
He was about to lose his job, and with it could go his invention. It now belonged to the company, and although he would get credit for it, and it would make

What Price Ambition?

him rich one day, he could not take it on to its conclusion himself. The
Company Chairman had been sympathetic, but at the end of the day, profits were his prime concern.
Antonio was not destitute. He had dabbled in the stock market, and was successful. He could afford to take a month or two off till he could get his head straight, and as he sat there in the empty silence, he knew what he would do. He would go home next month, and go to Italy to find his real self. Maybe his Grandmother would go with him. Then he would confront Mario with the truth.
There was nothing Mario could do to him. Antonio was fit and strong and a third his age. Then, he would return to Australia as a visitor, and help Drew get ready for the season. After that, he would make his own life in whatever direction looked good at the time.
He paused as he formulated his plans. He would need to do something about Dimitri Ferolla. Show him that he was not going to lie down and take it. Show him who was boss. The thought made Antonio's heart pound, not with fear, but with excitement. He would be pitting his wits against one of the most influential men in Europe. He, Antonio, against the Ferolla family, for he would undoubtedly be on his own. He could not count on any help from Mario, nor from his father. If they thought he was really in trouble, neither one would abandon him,

but they would not want to get involved in a battle of the Families.

His last few weeks in Australia were wild and abandoned, and he said goodbye to Drew and Rick with a heavy heart.

"I'm sorry, guys," he said as he stood at the airport with them, "Someone doesn't like me very much, but I'll be back. Keep at it, Drew. You're nearly there."

His Grandmother agreed immediately to go to Italy with him, despite opposition from Mario.

"What on earth do you want your Grandmother with you for, boy? A young man like you."

"She'll be my chaperone," replied Antonio, and then with a cheeky grin, he added, "Or I'll be hers. Nonna can still attract a glance or two."

Mario grunted in irritation, "That old woman," he said ungallantly, "Who would want her?"

"You'd be surprised," said Antonio in defence of his Grandmother whom he loved very much.

Even with Antonio's prejudiced eyes, Anna was an attractive, mature woman in her early sixties. Her hair was still raven black without any hint of grey. She was trim and elegant, with an immaculate dress sense. Anna had the presence she had always had as a girl, and she still turned a head or two when she went out.

Antonio saw the sense of adventure in her which had driven her into the arms of his real Grandfather. She would have been a Juliet, tragic and beautiful, except

What Price Ambition?

that she was a survivor. The very act of surviving through the horror and awful hurt she had suffered had nurtured the hate until it became an obsession with her. Mario was the object of that obsession. Mario who had wanted her enough to kill for her.
In Antonio's mind, Mario was the one he felt sorry for. Mario had given everything to Anna. In his own way, he had loved her more than anything else in the world. Even at Anna's own admission, Mario had put her on a pedestal, and worshipped her throughout their marriage. It did not seem right that Anna should repay his devotion with a growing hate.
Despite his fondness for Mario, who had always been the Grandpa he loved, he felt a bond with Anna, his natural Grandmother, and he resented Mario's derision.
"You'd better be nice to her, Grandpa," he said with a smile on his lips but which Mario knew was not reflected in his eyes, "She might decide to stay in Italy."
Mario glared at Antonio.
"She wouldn't dare. Anna knows her place."
Antonio heard the echo of the menace which must have sent a shiver through his Grandmother all those years ago.
"I'm joking, Grandpa. There's no way Nonna won't come back to you."
He looked directly at Mario hoping that Mario would somehow realise the truth behind then statement, and be

aware of the danger he could be in, but Mario only laughed.
He was too wrapped up in his own ego to feel threatened.
"You're right, Antonio. Your Nonna has always come running when I call. Have a good time."

Chapter 11.

Birthright.

Anna was quiet as the express train rattled through the valleys of Tuscany. They had flown to Rome, spent a few days there seeing the sights, and then on to their destination.

"It's very beautiful, Nonna," said Antonio, looking out of the windows.

Anna replied in Italian, her face absently reliving her youth, and Antonio looked at her in surprise. He knew some Italian for his father was bi-lingual, but they did not speak it regularly at home.

"Sorry, Antonio. For a minute I was back in Tuscany as a girl."

Antonio smiled, "And I bet you were beautiful then too." Anna smiled, "I had a good life. I had many young men calling at the restaurant to see me. They courted a woman in my day, Antonio, asking my father's permission to call, bringing me presents, behaving

impeccably. There was no free love in those days.
You had to be engaged before you could even let a man kiss your cheek."

"But you and Antonio, you were lovers. You must have been close friends before that."

"Yes, we were," admitted Anna, "That's what made it so exciting and romantic. We met in the garden of the inn where I lived. I used to climb out of my window to meet him. We were so much in love. We kissed under the cherry tree. I can still smell the blossom sometimes. I never kissed Mario till our wedding night. It was awful. All I could think about was my Antonio and the sweetness of his kisses. I hated Mario. I hated him near me."

She turned towards Antonio, "I've lived with that hate since then, waiting for the day he will pay for what he did."

"Nonna, I've not come to seek vengeance. I've told you, I have no grudges against Mario. He's always been my Grandpa. My mission this trip is to find my real family."

"It's not just your family, Antonio. It's your inheritance too. The Andresis are a wealthy family."

As Anna's words echoed in his head, Antonio's mind focused on the impact of what she was saying, Wealth, power. He needed both if he was to manoeuvre to a position of authority. The Andresi fortune would give him that.

What Price Ambition?

"But Dad is the rightful heir. He's the one with the right to claim the title. He's Count Giorgio Andresi."
"Yes, you're right, but your father won't want it. I know Giorgio. Anything for a quiet life. He won't want to rock the boat. He'll sign it over to you. We'll get the lawyers to sort it out. You *will* have it. You're so like your Grandfather, my Antonio."
"And what about Claudia. She's surely entitled to something."
Anna was silent for a moment.
"Yes, I suppose you're right. I'm sure we can sort out something. Don't you care for her at all, Antonio?"
Antonio was about to deny any affection for Claudia, but he could not form the words, for there in his head, was that warm feeling when he said her name. He looked out of the window and spoke to Anna's image reflected in the glass.
"I was horrified at first when I realised who she was. It was a hell of a shock, Nonna, The girl I had never met before I went to London was my cousin. I couldn't bear to be in the same room with her. I felt dirty, soiled by the trick fate had played on me. Now, I don't know. It's not Claudia's fault, She hasn't done anything wrong. Then there was the baby, I couldn't handle it. I think I've treated her badly."
"Yes, you have, Antonio. You've broken her heart, and she doesn't know why you don't want her any more."

What Price Ambition?

"I can't, Nonna. It's like going with Maria. She's my cousin too. We grew up together, like brother and sister, not lovers. I can't."
"Do you love her, Antonio?" said Anna softly.
"Yes, that's the trouble," Antonio admitted for the first time since he had found out the truth, "I love Claudia so much it hurts. I tried to deny it at first. To shut her out of my life, but you can't change the way you feel, can you Nonna?"
"No, you can't, but you don't love her enough to think of her as a person, and not just a product of her parentage. She's just another girl, Antonio. Cousins have married before, and her mother was only Giorgio's half sister. Look at the Royal Family."
"I can't risk it Nonna. What if our children were born with some defect because we were too closely related? I couldn't stand that."
"Antonio, where's your brain? Don't have any children if that's what's stopping you. Don't punish yourself and Claudia over something you can control. Goodness me, boy, life has enough twists you can't control without inventing more. If you want Claudia, take her for what she is."
Antonio got up and leaned his head against the carriage window, staring unseeing out at the sun-drenched countryside with its rolling fields full of ripening crops.
"Do you think   she'll still want me, Nonna?"

What Price Ambition?

His voice was so filled with pain that Anna's heart went out to him.

"I don't know, Antonio, but you won't find out by feeling sorry for yourself. Go and ask her yourself."

Antonio stood pressed against the window for several minutes. Maybe his Grandmother was right. He had been confusing the two issues, his love for Claudia as a woman with Claudia, his cousin. He had assumed that one day he would have children to carry on the Family name, but it wouldn't be the end of the world if he did not. Suddenly he laughed and turned round.

"You know, Nonna, I don't know what I'd do without your common sense. Everything came at me like a tornado out of the blue, and I just couldn't handle it. You're right, we don't have to have any children, and we could consult the best specialists if we do want to take the risk. I left her pregnant and alone, Nonna, and now she hasn't even got our baby. I forced her to get rid of it. I hope she can forgive me for that."

Anna smiled, "Nothing's impossible, Antonio, if you want it badly enough."

They took a taxi from Florence to the estate in the hills surrounding the old city. The families who ran it had kept it profitable and in order all these years, and they had been advised by the lawyers that they were coming. They were met with great excitement. The housekeeper and her husband chatted non-stop in Italian, and shook

What Price Ambition?

Antonio's hand, several times before they were ushered into the rambling old house.
Inside it was cool, its thick stone walls and small windows keeping out the sunlight. The furnishings were as old as the house. There were heavy oak dressers and tables with huge leather chairs into which Antonio sank gratefully to accept the glass of wine the maid offered.
"This is some place, Nonna."
Anna was wandering round the room, her face contorted with her painful memories.
"I was only here once," she whispered, "Antonio's father sent for me after he was killed. He knew what had happened, but he could do nothing against Mario. He was sympathetic, Antonio had told him about me, and he arranged for the marriage certificate to be buried in the chapel. After your father was born, he came to see me. Somehow he knew that Giorgio was his Grandson. He was an imposing man, regal, a man of few words.
"He will have my name." was all he said and touched your father's head with his finger. I thought at the time it was like the Pope blessing Giorgio. Well, The Count had papers drawn up, and a birth certificate produced for your father with his true parentage. It rests in the chapel with my marriage certificate, but of course the lawyers have copies. Your inheritance is waiting for you Antonio." and she raised her glass to him, "Count Antonio Andresi.

What Price Ambition?

You've come home, son."
"This is ridiculous, Nonna. No-one else knows. How can I inherit if you don't tell my father, and if he knows, Mario will know? And Claudia has to be told. Her father will know. Mario isn't going to like it."
"I don't care what Mario likes or doesn't like. You're all I care about. This is all yours. I've kept it for you all these years. It's time for it all to be settled."
"Okay, so let's get it done," said Antonio impatiently, "I want to get on with my life."
"All in good time. First you will see what your responsibilities will be from now on. It's a big responsibility, Antonio, and you will need a few days to seriously consider it. You can have anything you want, Antonio."
"I want Claudia. I want to go and see her, and try and right
the damage I've done."
"Very well. I'll find out where she is, and we'll go and see her in a few days. No arguments. Four days, Antonio."
"Yes, Nonna" said Antonio meekly, "Okay, milady. Show me what I am." he grinned.
Anna phoned Mario and the wheels of the Agusta Family were put into motion to find out where Claudia was. It was not difficult for she was in the Ferolla family stronghold in Sicily. It was no secret. There was

What Price Ambition?

no need to hide her identity or conceal her from anyone for she was in the bosom of her family and protected.
Mario was delighted that Antonio seemed to have come to his senses and did everything to help, unaware of the serpents which would be released as a result.
Antonio would not listen to Anna who wanted him to phone Claudia before he went to see her.
"No!" he said shortly, "I don't want her to run away from me. You stay here if you want."
They booked into a hotel in Palermo. The Ferolla village was only half a day's drive into the countryside from there, and Antonio hired a car. He went alone, despite Anna's protests.
Driving steadily along the dusty road on the approach to the village, the thought struck him that he was going back in time. Farming folk toiled in the fields, the women in their traditional black woollen frocks arid black scarves round their heads, and the men gnarled and withered from exposure to the elements. Life was simple and hard here, and many of the young people left to seek a better existence in the towns or the mainland.
The streets were deserted except for a few dogs lying in the shadows. It was the time when people rested out of the heat of the sun after their midday meal. The sound of the car engine was like an echo of thunder rumbling across the valley, and up the hillside where the village

What Price Ambition?

cringed in the shadow of a large protruding slope on which grew a few stunted trees.

Antonio stopped the car outside the church. If anyone knew where Claudia was, it would be the priest. He climbed out of the driver's seat slowly, and took off his sun glasses to look around. Then he leaned back into the car and picked up his jacket, slinging it across one shoulder. He could feel more than a dozen eyes staring at him from behind lace curtains, and he smiled, deliberately turning round so that they could get a good view.

The slam of the car door as he pushed it shut was like the crack of a bullet in the stillness, and Antonio leaped up the three steps to the old oak door of the church in its reverberation.

Inside, the church was cool and dimly lit. A shaft of sunlight filtered through a broken pane in the stained glass window, falling like a torch across the front pew. Antonio looked around. It was ornately carved, and gilded with statues and icons set into niches in the walls.

"Can I help you, Signor?" said a voice in Italian which made Antonio jump, for he had not seen the priest silently glide from the door into the aisle where Antonio stood.

Antonio replied in Italian.

"Yes, thank you, Monsignor, I'm looking for Claudia Ferolla. She's my fiancée."

What Price Ambition?

The priest considered his words for a second or two.
"You must be Antonio Agusta. Why did you come here? Don't you know the trouble you've caused that young woman?"
"Yes, Father, I do. God knows I do."
Antonio had never been religious, even although he had been brought up a strict Roman Catholic as a boy.
"God knows the truth, my son," said the priest, "Come. Sit. Tell me your story."
Antonio hesitated. He was not sure how much Claudia had told this priest, and he did not want to add fuel to his righteous attitude.
"If you don't mind, father, I would rather see Claudia first. I need to tell her I'm sorry and beg her forgiveness."
"If you truly repent, God will forgive you the sins you committed, and I'm sure Claudia will not argue with God's will, but I don't know if she will want to see you, my son." Before Antonio could reply, the door of the church was pushed open vigorously, and it banged against the wall. Two identically dressed men in black suits walked briskly down the aisle towards them.
"Who is he, Father?" said one.
The priest told them.
"Thank you, Father, " said the other, "We'll take care of Mr. Agusta."

What Price Ambition?

He took Antonio's arm in a grip like steel, and Antonio's natural reaction was to resist, but he thought better of it, and decided to do what they suggested.
"Okay, guys, no hassle," he said in English, but the two men just stared at him stonily.
"God be with you, my son," said the priest as they took him out into the brilliant sunshine again. Antonio hoped that he would have some influence in that department, even for lapsed worshippers like him.
His worst fears became reality when he was pushed through a door of a house opposite the church, and he stumbled to his knees with the force. Before he could get up, one of the men kicked him in the side of his ribs, and Antonio cried out in agony. He heard the crack and felt the pain when his ribs broke, but he did not have time to think about it because the other man pulled his head back by his hair.
"The Don wants to talk to you, Agusta," he said in English, and he pushed Antonio flat on the cold stone floor, "Just remember your manners."
They both pulled him to his feet, and Antonio clutched his ribs as they propelled him to the far side of the hall and through a door.
The room, in contrast to the cool, dark hall, was bright and colourful. It's pastel shades were highlighted by the sun streaming through French windows which opened on to a terrace.

What Price Ambition?

Seated at a table, his head bowed over some papers, was a grey-haired man, and Antonio thought he looked familiar. The man did not even look at him when the two men stood Antonio in front of the desk, themselves silently at attention.
Antonio could not stand it any longer.
"What is this?" he said, and almost passed out with another wave of pain, as he was hit in the side of the head.
"Shut up," said the man who had hit him.
Antonio doubled over, in too much pain to say anything else, but he saw the grey head lift slowly, and when he recovered enough to straighten up, he was looking into the deep, dark eyes which showed no compassion.
"Leave him!" the man ordered in Italian, "You speak, Italian?".
Antonio nodded, still catching his breath to ride the pain, "A little. Who are you?"
The man put down the pen he was holding, and leaned back in his chair.
"I'm Giuseppe Ferolla, the head of the Family."
He swept his hand in an arc in front of him, and Antonio knew he meant more than just in the village.
"You're Dimitri Ferolla's father,"
The man smiled wryly, "Yes, Claudia's Grandfather. You've been a very wicked young man, Antonio Agusta," he said and raised his forefinger, "My

What Price Ambition?

Nipotina is very unhappy, and you've dishonoured your own Grandfather. You've broken your promise."
"Yes Sir, I'm sorry," said Antonio, "But I've come to put it right, I love Claudia. I need to talk to her. There's something she doesn't know."
Giuseppe Ferolla shrugged, "Maybe later, but sorry isn't good enough. You've deliberately insulted a Ferolla. I can't allow you to walk away from here unpunished."
Antonio's heart quickened. He could only imagine the worst, and he was suddenly afraid. His Grandmother had been right. He should not have come alone.
Giuseppe nodded to the two men, and they grabbed Antonio's arms again. This time he struggled, but it was no use. He could not shake them off, and the pain in his ribs and his head came over him in waves with a wash of nausea the more he struggled.
"Please, Let me just see Claudia." he cried desperately as they dragged him away, but the old man said nothing.
They took him down some steps to a cellar, and tied his hands together before they hoisted him up on a rope slung across an oak beam till his toes were just off the floor. Antonio dangled at the end of the rope, and turned round like a plumb-line. His arms were already feeling hot and sore as if they were about to be wrenched out of their sockets, and the pain was excruciating as the muscles in his chest were stretched to the full.

What Price Ambition?

"See how you like hanging around, Agusta," said one man, "Senorina Ferolla does nothing else all day."
They left and shut the door behind them. The room fell into a gloomy darkness when they switched the light off, for there were no windows, and Antonio gritted his teeth in mental and physical agony. He tried to swing his body and maybe loosen the rope enough to reach the floor, but all he succeeded in doing was to tighten the knots round his wrist.
"Come on, Antonio," he said to himself, "There must be something you can do."
He tried to pull himself up, but he could not get his hand round the rope, and he fell back with a cry of defeat when the effort made him sweat. After a while he gave up. His hands were numb anyway and he had crossed the pain barrier to numb his senses too. His head dropped to his chest, and he lost consciousness for a few minutes.
It could have been longer, for he had no sensation of time, but he came to with a start when a shaft of light crept slowly across the floor. It seemed an eternity before the door opened, and Antonio held his breath. He knew it could not be the two men back again. They would not have been so reticent to enter.
If it was some other sort of torture he wanted to be ready for it. Then he heard her cry.
"Antonio! Oh, god, Antonio!"

What Price Ambition?

It was Claudia. She ran forward and threw her arms round him.
"Claudia," he croaked, "I'm sorry. I'm really sorry."
Claudia was crying as she considered what to do, "Don't talk, Antonio," she sobbed, "Just a minute."
She found the light switch and looked around. There were some chests in one corner, and she dragged one of them over, and pushed it underneath Antonio to take the weight off his arms.
Antonio cried out in agony when the blood started to circulate again into his numb limbs. The pain was more than he could bear.
"What is it?" said Claudia in alarm, tears streaming down her face, "Shall I take it away?"
"No!" gasped Antonio, "It will be alright in a minute. Can you find something to cut the rope, Sweetheart?"
Claudia searched again and found a rusty pair of garden shears. She dragged another chest next to Antonio and stood on it. Antonio was filled with a sweetness which even subdued the pain when she stood next to him, her body touching his.
She hugged him briefly, and then set about sawing at the rope with the shears.
It took some time, and her arms ached, but Claudia kept on till suddenly the frayed rope was cut through. She quickly did the other hand, and Antonio tumbled to the floor in a heap as his legs gave way, The pain was just too much for him. When he came to a second time,

What Price Ambition?

Claudia was cradling his head in her lap, and she stroked his bruised face.
"My poor baby," she whispered, "They shouldn't have done this to you. I'm sorry, Antonio."
Antonio tried to smile, but it hurt too much, and he closed his eyes.
"I deserve it, Claudia," he said in a barely audible voice, "It's nothing to what I did to you. I was cruel, and I'm sorry."
"It doesn't matter now, Antonio. I've got you back. You *did* come to find me, didn't you?"
"Yes, we need to talk."
"Later. Look, I'm going to see my Grandfather to get you upstairs. Don't go away."
Antonio smiled weakly, "I don't think I can," he said as she squeezed his hand and left the room.
Some of the household staff came and carried him to a clean, comfortable bed and Claudia bathed his wounds.
"This time you can't run away," she laughed, "You have a nice body, Antonio. I've dreamed about you every night, wishing I was in your arms again."
Claudia, don't," he said and caught her hand, "There's something you have to know. You might not want to see me again when I tell you."
He held on to her hand and told her about his Grandmother and his natural Grandfather for whom he was named, and who was also Claudia's Grandfather.

What Price Ambition?

"So, you see, Claudia, your mother and my father are brother and sister. That night in Australia when you told me who your mother was, I freaked out. I couldn't come to terms with it."
"Half brother and sister," corrected Claudia, "They had different mothers, but what difference does that make to us, Antonio?"
Antonio stared at her, "We're cousins, Claudia."
"Does that make any difference?" she asked and her face was sweet and innocent, "I love you, Antonio, and I know you love me."
"I don't suppose it does to us. I thought it did at first, Claudia. That's why I ran away, but now... I just know I can't live without you...It might not be possible to have children." he added.
Claudia bent her head, "I had a baby, Antonio," she whispered, "They took it away from me. I know it was perfect."
Antonio pulled her to him, "I'm sorry Sweetheart. I know you've got no reason to forgive me, but I really am sorry. I was cruel and heartless. Oh Claudia, I love you."
She fell against him and he winced at the pain, but he held her tight.
"I don't care about children, Antonio. I don't want to think about it. I just want you."
"I love you, Claudia. I'll never leave you again."

What Price Ambition?

"Grandfather won't let you," she said with a laugh, "He didn't really mean to hurt you, Antonio. He loves me very much."

"I'd hate to be on the receiving end when he does mean it then. We're going to have to confront our parents with this. Mario's going to take it badly."

"But does he need to know the truth?"

"I want to claim my inheritance."

He did not want to hide anything else from her, and he told her about his visit to the family estates.

"But, isn't Mario's inheritance enough for you?"

Antonio frowned. How could he tell her that he was going to be the most powerful figure in Europe, or about his own vows to pay her father back for his part in trying to bring Mario down.

He had broken his vow to be honest with her in the matter of a few seconds, but he quickly rationalised it by telling himself that there were some things Claudia did not need to know.

"It isn't enough for my plans. You know, the racing game."

Claudia smiled, "You've got huge ambitions, Antonio. I'll help you. I'll be a good wife for you."

"Sure you will, Sweetheart. We're good together."

He breathed deeply with relief that Claudia had not pursued it further, and they sat holding hands and discussed their predicament.

What Price Ambition?

Claudia trusted him and that was good. He would take care of her and protect her from things she would be better not to know. Italian women were used to that, and Claudia would be no different to his mother or Grandmother. He was the head of the Family. She would do her duty as his wife. That was the way of it.

Chapter 12.

Confrontation.

As they sat together holding hands, Antonio and Claudia suddenly heard shouting downstairs.
"What's going on?" said Antonio trying to sit up.
"No, you can't. You can't move, Antonio. You're hurt."
Antonio tried once more but he fell back on the pillows, his breath rasping and heavy.
"Shit!" he hissed between clenched teeth, "I can't get up. I haven't got the strength. Christ, Claudia, I'm no more than a baby lying here."
Claudia smiled, "You're my baby, Antonio. I'll take care of you. Wait here. I'll see what's causing the commotion down there."
Before Antonio could say anything, Claudia hurried from the room, and ran lightly down the wide staircase which led to the hall. Just as she reached the bottom step, the door burst open and four men pushed into the house, shouting to everyone to stand still.
"Where's Ferolla?" said one of the men.

What Price Ambition?

"No!" cried Claudia and stepped forward from the shadow of the staircase where she had been poised. One of the men swung round immediately and fired the gun he was holding.
Claudia took a few stilted steps like a puppet, and collapsed face down on the tiled floor. The housekeeper screamed and   rushed to her side without any regard for her own safety.
"Mama mia! You've hilled the child. Senore Ferolla, they've killed Claudia!"
There was another crash as a door from the rear of the house burst open, and Giuseppe's men flooded in. It was difficult to say how many there were as they piled through en masse, but it was certainly enough to overrun the place. The four men who had started the attack fired several shots which miraculously did not do any serious damage, before they fled from the house. Giuseppe pushed his way through the throng of bodies, barking orders before he crossed to the stairs and knelt beside Claudia where the housekeeper was trying to stop the bleeding. said.
"Is she dead?"
The housekeeper sobbed, "No, Patron, she's still breathing but the blood. Mama di deus, the poor child is bleeding to death."
Giuseppe he took his wallet from his inside pocket,
 "Press this on the wound and hold it there. Firmly now, Maria, as hard as you can.

What Price Ambition?

The blood soaked the tan leather, and the notes inside it but it did the trick, and the bleeding was stemmed after a few minutes.
The doctor was there before the ambulance and he did what he could till they could get Claudia to hospital.
All the time Antonio lay upstairs in frustration. He had heard the shots and the screams, and when Claudia did not return, his heart was beating with a black dread fast enough to explode. Eventually, he tumbled out of bed, and pulled himself to the top of the stairs.
"Senora!" he called as a maid cleaned the blood away, "What's happened? Where's Claudia?"
The maid jumped up with start, "Senorina Claudia is hurt, Sir. She was shot. She might die."
She crossed herself and called a male member of the household to help her see to Antonio.
Two men got him back into bed where he struggled to sit up. Tears ran down his face as he pleaded with them to take him to Claudia, but they called the doctor and he gave him a sedative.
"Please God, don't let her die," he whispered as he drifted into unconsciousness.
When he awoke, it was dark and the room was still. His head was spinning with the hangover the drugs had left, but he felt stronger despite that. He managed to sit up and switch on the bedside light, and all at once the memory came back to him, and his heart lurched with the agony of it. With an effort, he pulled himself

What Price Ambition?

painfully from the bed to the chair where his clothes had been neatly placed. After a few minutes rest to get his breath, he got dressed, but it took him a full half hour, and afterwards, he lay back in the armchair exhausted with the effort. The skies were turning grey by then, and Antonio knew it must be morning, but in fact it was two days later. He had slept fitfully for nearly forty eight hours.

When he felt strong enough, and the blood had stopped rushing to his head, he stood up unsteadily and made his way slowly to the stairs. It seemed a long way down, and he leaned on the banister for a second. Then he sat down on the first step and negotiated the rest like a young child at its first attempt.

He was almost at the bottom when Giuseppe appeared in the hall, but Antonio was concentrating so much, that he did not see him till Giuseppe spoke.

"So, you're feeling better, Antonio. Where are you going?"

"I'm going to Claudia. You can't stop me," he added defiantly.

"I don't think I'll need to. You won't get far in that state, young man."

"How is she?"

"She's stable but still critical," said Giuseppe and Antonio realised he was speaking perfect English. However, he let it pass without comment, and tried to pull himself up.

What Price Ambition?

"I want to see her."

Giuseppe looked at him stonily.

"And why would you want to see my Granddaughter?"

"Because I love her, Mr. Ferolla. Surely she told you."

"Yes, she told me, but my eyes tell me something different."

"What do you mean? What do I have to do to prove it?"

"The men who shot Claudia were your Grandfather's men," said Giuseppe coldly, "You're an Agusta too. From the same mould. You've proved already that you're not to be trusted."

"No, I'm not. I'm *not* an Agusta."

The thought that Mario had attempted to murder Claudia or any of her family sickened him.

Giuseppe tilted his head enquiringly, "Not an Agusta?" he said in surprise, "But Mario is your Grandfather. His son, Giorgio is your father."

"No!...no, Mario isn't my natural Grandfather," Antonio said softly, and sat down on the stairs, "My father was conceived before my Grandmother married Mario. She had a brief relationship with another man, even married him. Mario killed him... Antonio Andresi."

"Andresi!" exclaimed Giuseppe, "Count Alberto Andresi's son, The Baron in north Tuscany. I heard about the killing. They said it was a hunting accident."

"Murder, more like. Mario gunned him down in my Grandmother's arms as they lay together on their wedding night. Mario did not know they had been secretly married. She never told him, and the only other person who knew was Count Alberto."

"So, if this is true, you and Claudia are related. Did you know her mother is also an Andresi?"

Antonio nodded, "Yes, I found out and that's why I ran away. I couldn't handle it at first. It seemed so unreal, almost as if it was wrong."

"I see," said Giuseppe, "And you couldn't tell Claudia for fear of Mario. It's all clear now."

"Not just that. I loved Mario. He's the only Grandfather I've known. I didn't want to hurt him."

"So why did you change your mind and come looking for Claudia?"

"Nonna made me see that my feelings for Claudia were the only important issues, I had to talk to her and tell her the truth. Then, if she still wanted me, we could expose the lies and be together. It's not illegal for cousins to marry."

"No, not usual, but not illegal either, and your father, does he know all this?"

"No, Sir, he doesn't. Nonna says he won't want the Andresi inheritance."

"And you do?"

"Of course. Wouldn't you?"

Giuseppe smiled, "Probably and Claudia didn't mind when you told her."

What Price Ambition?

"No, she said it didn't matter. We were just deciding what to do when,., please let me see her." pleaded Antonio,
Giuseppe stepped forward and held out his hand to Antonio,
"I think we should have some breakfast first, and then we'll go together to see her. It's too early to disturb her at the hospital."
Giuseppe called for his staff, and they bustled around lighting a fire against the chill of the morning, and preparing coffee and food for the two of them.
When the sun started to warm the land, they left the house, and were driven to Palermo to see Claudia. Antonio stopped at the door when the nurse showed him to the private room where she lay pale and still, wired like a machine to the monitors and transfusions. Her eyes were closed, and she looked like a porcelain doll as she lay unmoving except for the regular heaving of her chest as she breathed in her subconscious state.
"Claudia, what has he done to you?" Antonio whispered.
He clenched his fists, for he was almost blinded by the rage which enveloped him. Mario had done this, just as he had killed Beccy, He, Antonio, had become once more the unwilling accomplice at Mario's whim.
"What did he think he was achieving?" he said out loud.

What Price Ambition?

"They were sent to look for you with orders to kill anyone who got in the way, but they were fools. They bungled it." said Giuseppe.
"Yes, and so has Mario. He'll pay for this. I'll kill him if she dies."
Giuseppe put his hand on Antonio's shoulder.
"He's already a marked man."
"No!" said Antonio fiercely, "He's mine. Let me avenge Claudia, Mr. Ferolla. She will be *my* wife."
Giuseppe nodded, "You have it, my boy. Go with God, Antonio, and be careful. Mario Agusta is a ruthless man."
"Don't I know it," said Antonio, and he lifted Claudia's hand, "I'd like to sit with her for a while."
Giuseppe left him alone with her.
After Antonio's visit, Claudia seemed to gather an inner strength, and she started to come round. It took several days for her to completely regain consciousness, but when she finally opened her eyes, Antonio was at her bedside. She smiled at him, and whispered his name, and he lifted her hand to his lips.
"Sweetheart, thank god you're okay."
"I dreamt we got married, Antonio," she said, as if she had just woken up from a night's sleep, "It was a beautiful wedding."
"And it will be, Claudia. As soon as you're well, I'm going to marry you. I love you Claudia."

What Price Ambition?

Antonio too had recovered from the beating he took, and there was only slight bruising visible on his face. In the days he waited for Claudia to recover, he had contacted his Grandmother to tell her he was alright, and persuaded her to go home to Mario.
He was going home himself in a few days, although he was not sure what he was going to say to Mario.
In the event, it was all laid out for Antonio when his father met him at the airport.
"You're Grandfather's in a foul mood," Giorgio said, "It seems you've been causing a few headaches, Antonio, and my mother has summoned me to their house. Do you know what she wants?"
Antonio glanced at his father. He guessed what Anna would be saying to him.
She had hinted as much in Italy, but he was not going to be the one to tell his father.
"No, I haven't got a clue, Dad. Grandpa shouldn't have got involved. I can take care of myself."
His father did not say anything, for he had always tried to keep out of the family business. The whole thing made him uneasy, and although he had taken what it had given him and enjoyed the good things in life because of his connections, he did not approve of some of the methods used to achieve it.
Giorgio knew that Mario interfered in everyone's life from his own bitter experience and he was sure that Antonio was no exception.

What Price Ambition?

However, Antonio had other ideas, and he strode through his Grandfather's house purposefully.
"Nonna," he said and kissed her cheek, "Where's Grandpa?"
"Out in the garden, Antonio. What are you going to do?"
"Tell him the truth."
"Then it's time. Come Giorgio, we must talk." she said and took her eldest son's arm, and walked with him into the sitting room.
Mario was pruning his roses, and he looked up with a smile when he saw Antonio.
"So, you've returned in one piece and alone. What were you thinking of Antonio. That Ferolla girl has addled your brain, it's was good that you tried to make peace with her, but to walk into their stronghold on your own is just foolishness."
"We're getting married. Just as soon as Claudia is well enough."
Mario stopped attending to the flowers and straightened up.
"You can't marry her now, Antonio. I forbid it. They tried to kill you. Why the change of heart anyway? Last time we spoke you were adamant that you didn't want her."
Antonio felt himself get angry, but he controlled his urge to shout at Mario.

What Price Ambition?

"I *am* marrying Claudia, Grandpa," he said softly restraining the urge to raise his voice, "And I don't need your permission for anything I do."
Mario looked at Antonio in surprise but he ignored his outburst,
"Come, Antonio, let's go and sit on the patio. I'll get some wine."
He poured the rich Barolo into two glasses,.
"I want to explain something to you, son, something you will have to accept when all this is yours. We made an enemy when you rejected Claudia Ferolla. We had a contract with her father. *We* broke it. They cannot ignore that. It's like laying down the gauntlet, like saying that their family is not good enough for an Agusta. You understand Antonio. We have insulted them, taken their honour, and worse, dishonoured their daughter. It was a good sign that you wanted to see her, but they rejected your attempt at an apology by kidnapping you, so now it's too late for reconciliation."
Antonio listened without once interrupting Mario, and he was aware that his Grandfather not once blamed him directly for the situation they were in now, referring always to it as a Family problem.
"But surely if Claudia and I can forgive and forget, the two families can too. Her Grandfather doesn't have any objections now."
Mario shook his head sadly, "It's too late, Antonio. The vendetta has begun. Dimitri is moving in on our Far

What Price Ambition?

East business with renewed vigour, and he's started a territorial war with our London interests. It's past time for negotiating, so you see I cannot allow you to join with any member of his Family."
Antonio put down his glass abruptly.
"I told you, Grandpa, I'm marrying Claudia. I don't give a damn about your family feuds. You can keep the Family tradition if that's what it means."
"You are the Agusta heir, Antonio," Mario said quietly, "You cannot ignore your birthright."
Antonio looked directly at Mario.
"And what if it isn't my birthright? What if I've inherited it falsely?"
Mario stared at him in silence, not knowing what he meant, but sensing that Antonio was deadly serious. Antonio went on before Mario could say anything.
"I'm not of your blood, Mario," he said briefly, deliberately using a stylized formal language, "I'm not an Agusta."
"Don't be ridiculous. You're Giorgio's son. I was there minutes after you were born."
Antonio leaned forward, "But Giorgio isn't *your* son."
Mario slapped him once across his cheek, and Antonio closed his eyes, and heard the anguish in the other man's voice. The man who was his beloved Grandfather.
"How dare you, Antonio. How dare you insult your Grandmother like that."

What Price Ambition?

Antonio looked at Mario defiantly, "Giorgio is Antonio Andresi's son. Nonna was pregnant when she married you."

Mario suddenly flopped back in the chair as if he had been struck, and his eyes took on a look of defeat for a second. Then Antonio saw the thunder gather and force its way to the surface.

Mario sat up and thumped the table, making the glasses jump and the wine spill on to the surface.

"So, Andresi has won after all," he said bitterly, "You have his eyes. I remember the look he gave me when he died. Did she tell you it all?"

Antonio nodded, and suddenly he felt sorry for Mario.

"Look, Grandpa, you've always been good to me. I love you, but I'm not an Agusta. Maybe you should give it to Uncle Sergio."

Mario laughed bitterly, "Sergio!" he sneered, "He couldn't run an errand let alone the family business. I don't want this to go any further, Antonio. Promise me. You're still my Grandson, and you will take over from me."

"There's more, Grandpa," said Antonio, and this time he hung his head as he told Mario about Claudia's involvement.

"And her Grandfather, Giuseppe knows. So, they have another rod to use on my back. Well, there can be no contract. This Family will not join with the Ferollas, not now, not ever. Do I make myself clear, Antonio? You're

What Price Ambition?

part of this family whether you like it or not. Now, if you'll excuse me, I have to see your Grandmother."
Antonio stood up abruptly and made way for Mario, the Grandfather who was not.
He admired the man at that moment. He had dignity in his hurt and Antonio loved him despite his attempts to deny it.
"Grandpa I..." he began, and Mario turned to look at him, his eyes haunted by the past.
"Nothing," said Antonio, and looked away, unable to tell Mario how he felt.
He watched as Mario disappeared into the house, and he was still standing there when his father came into the garden.
"He knows." said Antonio, and sat down.
"I know he does." said Giorgio, who had cringed under Mario's look as they passed in the hallway, "He's with your Nonna now."
"He won't hurt her will he?"
Giorgio shook his head, "No, I don't think so. He loves her, Antonio."
Giorgio poured himself some wine, and smiled without mirth, "How does it feel to be heir to a title, son?"
"No different. A few words don't make the man. I love Grandpa, Dad. I'll always think of him as my Grandfather."
"Yes, and he's always been a father to me," said Giorgio, "Even when I didn't want to follow in his

footsteps, but we're not his flesh and blood, I don't know how he'll take that. Not easily, you can be sure."
However, they were wrong. Mario accepted it without question.
"So what now, old woman?" he said when he was alone with Anna, "What have you proved by telling them? I want Antonio to have it all. He's the only one who is anything like me. That's a laugh, isn't it? Anna, how could you keep it from me?"
"I was afraid. I thought you would kill my baby."
"Anna, Anna, I could never do anything to hurt you." He shook his head sadly.
"That's a good one coming from you, Mario. You destroyed my life when you killed Antonio. I loved him. Do you hear! Love! Love! Something *you* will never understand."
Her voice rose in a crescendo of hate as she threw the accusing words at him.
"I've always loved you, Anna," said Mario quietly, "I thought you were just infatuated with Andresi. I thought he was just using you. I wanted you, I took what I wanted. We've had a good life, Anna. You've never wanted for anything."
"Except for one thing," said Anna sharply, "I wanted *you* dead. I've hated you all these years. Hated every minute with you."

What Price Ambition?

"I don't believe you, Anna," said Mario, and she knew he was hurt by her words, "We've had three children together. You were always willing."
Anna turned away from him, for if she was honest, she had developed a fondness for Mario. He had been gentle with her, showing her tenderness that no-one else knew, except maybe Antonio.
"You've destroyed us, Anna," Mario said wearily, "Is that what you really wanted. You hated me so much that you've destroyed your Grandson."
"Antonio will be fine. He's an Andresi. He'll inherit the family wealth and title from Giorgio."
Mario sat down abruptly and put his head in his hands. "So, what now?" he said, and he looked up quickly at Anna, "What now, woman? How are you going to put it all back together again? My business is threatened, my life in ruins. What now?"
Anna frowned. She was not sure any more. She had lived each day of her life with the hope that one day Antonio's murder would be avenged, but now she was hesitating. Did she really want Mario dead?
Mario did not wait for her to make up her mind, and he rose swiftly from the chair and crossed to the phone.
"Nicholas, I want to see you now. I have work for you."
He turned back to Anna, and she saw the fire in his eyes.
"I'm damned if I'll let it all go down the tube. Yes, maybe I will be damned. I'm past caring."

What Price Ambition?

"What are you going to do?" whispered Anna in fear.
"I'm not going to let Ferolla take what's mine. Antonio will not marry that girl."
Anna put her hands to her face in terror.
"No, Mario! You can't! Antonio loves her. He's your Grandson..." she stopped in mid sentence, "I'm sorry," she whispered, "This is my fault. They could have married happily not knowing the truth."
"Yes, they could, but your vicious thirst for revenge has put paid to that. He will *not* marry her, and I don't want you interfering. Now, let's go out there together, and show them that you're still my wife."
Anna stared at Mario as he held out his hand, but she took it without a word.
Her heart was full of dread, for Antonio whom she loved more than any of the others, was about to lose the one he loved, just as she had done. Anna knew it was no idle threat. Mario would destroy Claudia Ferolla one way or another before he would let her marry Antonio, and she was too afraid to stop him.
Antonio and Giorgio looked at one another as Mario came out with Anna, and waited for him to speak.
Mario smiled slowly, "It makes no difference. You see, we are still as we were."
He held up Anna's hand on which the gold wedding ring was clearly visible, "It changes nothing, Antonio. You claim your birthright by all means. That will make you twice as rich, twice as powerful. That's good. We

will fight for our family together. Let's hear no more of it. I have some business to attend to, so, if you'll both excuse me. Giorgio, we'll be over for lunch on Sunday as usual. I thought we might get in a round of golf first if you fancy it."

Yes, Dad," said Giorgio, "That will be great."

Antonio could not believe his ears. Nothing had changed. Mario was still manipulating everyone to his will.

"I'm sorry, Grandpa, but I can't just ignore all this. I'm going nowhere with my life. Following you like a lost sheep. I have my own plans."

"Yes, and you'll succeed, Antonio. By the way, they're testing your RAD modification next month, that's six months ahead of schedule."

Antonio looked at his Grandfather, "They didn't tell me." he said quietly.

"You weren't here. I spoke to Morrow yesterday, and Rick is to race next season. So, you see, Antonio, things are never as bad as they seem. Your Grandpa is good for something, isn't that right?"

"Yes," said Antonio quietly, "Thanks, Grandpa. I didn't expect results so quickly."

"When you're an Agusta, you rely on quick results and you should learn that lesson well, Antonio. It will save you a lot of grief later. Now, off you go, and do what you young men do these days, Chill out, isn't it, Relax a little. Put some fun into your life."

What Price Ambition?

Antonio knew he was dismissed, just like any other subject of the Don, but he checked the rush of angry words which cascaded from his head. Visions of his dream becoming reality tempered his protests. His Grandfather had come up with the right carrot to keep him in line once more.
"Sure, I'll see you later, Dad."
He said goodbye to his Grandmother, not really noticing her reluctance to hold any sort of conversation with him, and he ran down the steps to his car where the Family body guard opened the door for him.
"Have a good evening, Sir," the man said and shut the door.
Antonio was just pulling away on the main road when he looked in his rear mirror. A car was turning into the driveway behind him. He was sure it was Nicholas Derwent, and his blood churned through his heart at the thought. He disliked Derwent, not only for his part in destroying Beccy, but because he despised the dirty business Derwent was in. He stopped the car suddenly at the kerb of the wide tree-lined avenue. Derwent worked for Mario. It was his business Derwent was controlling. That made it Antonio's too, The realisation had at last penetrated his senses. He, Antonio Agusta, or even Andresi would be responsible for everything employees like Derwent did. Mario had ordered Beccy's death. He was sure of it, just as he had ordered the attack on

What Price Ambition?

Claudia's Italian home. Antonio could not accept that he had not intended to hurt Claudia. Mario had ultimately been responsible, and he, Antonio, was also responsible.

Antonio could not accept that burden of guilt. He would be expected to sit in judgment of the people who touched his life, and he would have the power to destroy them if he chose. He shuddered, remembering Julie Li Chang. He did not want anyone dead. He did not hate anyone that much. Mario and he were alike in many ways, but Antonio did not have the older man's ruthless sense of justice.

As he sat and contemplated the self-revelation, he would have been even more horrified and angry if he had heard how far Mario was prepared to go.

"Come in, Nick," Mario said to Nicholas Derwent, "I've got a job for you, and I don't want any hiccoughs. I want you to arrange an accident for Claudia Ferolla. There must be no doubt that it was nothing more than a tragic accident."

"Sure thing, Mr. Agusta. That's not, difficult. Where is she?"

"She's still in Italy, but she'll be back in England next week."

"Okay, leave it to me. You can order the wreath now."

Antonio was oblivious to all this, and phoned Claudia every day, sometimes twice a day. He was also making plans to return to Australia on a visitor's visa to be with

What Price Ambition?

his friends when Nick raced the car with their invention. He was hoping that Claudia would go with him, and he would be able to make it up to her. His deep feelings for her had returned, and he was no longer troubled by their blood relationship.

His father, Georgia, claimed his birth-right, and it was dragged through the Italian courts to establish him as Count Andresi. Antonio would inherit the title from him one day.

Claudia's mother was to be given a fair settlement as Giorgio's half-sister, and the two of them met in London for the first time as siblings. Prior to that, Josephina Ferolla had been only Antonio's fiancée's mother.

Her husband, Dimitri, was not present. He was still smarting over Antonio's treatment of Claudia, taking it as a personal insult which could not be forgiven easily. However, he loved his only daughter, and Claudia was working on his emotions to bring about the change which would embrace Antonio into the family.

The first indications that the vendetta had been relaxed was a phone call from the Australian embassy to tell Antonio to reapply for a work permit. Antonio was delighted, and his planned visit to Australia became something more permanent. He would marry Claudia before they went.

What Price Ambition?

His mother and father were delighted when he told them his intentions, as was his Grandmother, but Mario's face was like thunder.
"Antonio, I expressly forbade you to see this girl, and marriage is just out of the question," he said stiffly, like the reincarnation of a Victorian patriarch.
"Grandpa, you're getting too old," said Antonio defiantly, intending to dig at Mario where it might hurt most. He saw the tightening of the flesh at the corners of Mario's mouth, and his heart beat faster, "Dimitri Ferolla is prepared to forgive and forget, why can't you?" he went on before Mario could say anything, "Enough!" thundered Mario, "Who do you think you are, boy? If I tell you no, then that is exactly what you do. Do you understand, Antonio?"
Antonio took a deep breath. He had never openly defied his Grandfather before, and he had to muster all his strength of character to face him.
"Oh yes, I understand alright," he said quicker than he intended, "I'll say it again, you're getting past it, Grandpa. We need to compromise on some things, and negotiate a solution on others, Dimitri doesn't want to take your business away from you. I've been making some enquiries of my own. He would be happy to share the Far East with you. I had a long talk with Claudia's Grandfather, you and he have a lot in common. Dimitri will lift the vendetta on this family for one concession. I'm sorry I got you into it. It was my fault, and I told

What Price Ambition?

Giuseppe Ferolla just that. He understood, Grandpa. Why won't you? Look at it this way if you like. I've come up trumps anyway. I have the Agusta empire, the Andresi fortune, a foot in the Ferolla camp, and I've got the girl."

He laughed uneasily trying to make light of it.

Mario hesitated for only a second, "Not yet you haven't, boy," he said softly, "I said enough, Antonio. You know nothing about honour. How could you with your history. You're right, it is your fault I'm losing everything. Yours and your Grandmother's. She might even get her wish to see me dead, but I will *not* give up everything to the Ferollas without a fight. Do you understand, boy?"

Antonio nodded, "I understand, Grandpa. I just wish you did," and he turned away. He did not see the look of sorrow cross Mario's face, nor the slight step forward he took as if to reach out to Antonio.

"Okay, Grandpa," said Antonio over his shoulder as he went out, "Have it your way, but don't interfere in my life. I'm marrying Claudia, and there's nothing you can do about it. She's coming home in two days, and I plan to take her to Australia within the month."

Antonio left the room and went to see his Grandmother. "He's gone crazy, Nonna. He can't see past his nose on this one."

"Be careful, Antonio. Leopards don't change their spots. Mario can be ruthless."

What Price Ambition?

She put her hand on Antonio's arm, "Take Claudia out of here as soon as you can."
"I intend to Nonna. I think we'll be happier in Australia."

What Price Ambition?

Chapter 13.

The Way of It.

Antonio was desperate to see Claudia, but he resisted rushing to London so that she could have some time with her family. However, when the weekend approached, he could no longer contain himself, and flew to see her.

"Come in Antonio," said Claudia's mother and she hugged him, "We didn't expect you till Monday, but it's lovely to see you. What a business this has been." She confided in him quietly as she put her arm through his and guided him inside.

Antonio put his other hand on hers, "Yes, life's strange, isn't it. We should have known one another a long time ago. I should have grown up calling you Aunt. You don't mind about Claudia and me?"

"No, I don't mind," said Josephina Ferolla, "As long as you love her, Antonio."

Antonio smiled and she took him through to the conservatory where Claudia was having coffee with her father. Dimitri stood up when they entered.

What Price Ambition?

"I'm sorry, Mr. Ferolla," said Antonio at once.
He had no idea what to expect.
"You've caused this family a lot of grief, Antonio, but let's put it behind us. Come and join us and we can talk."
He held out his hand to Antonio, and he shook it firmly before he looked past Dimitri to where Claudia sat propped up on a couch. He smiled uncertainly at her, and she returned his look with warmth in her eyes which filled Antonio with a tenderness he had never experienced before.
"You look wonderful, Sweetheart. Are you alright?" he added anxiously.
Claudia laughed lightly, "I'm fine, Antonio. I'm just humouring Dad. He thinks I should be treated like a baby."
"He's quite right. You need to be looked after. I'm sorry, Claudia. I wouldn't have let this happen for anything. I wish I could put the clock back. I didn't handle any of it very well."
"Don't. Like Dad says, it's in the past, and we've got a future to look forward to together. Haven't you got something to say to me?"
"Sorry." said Antonio with a grin.
"No, silly. Grandfather tells me that you're planning a wedding. Don't I have a say in that?"
Antonio's eyes twinkled mischievously, "And why should you?" he said with a laugh.

What Price Ambition?

"Antonio Agusta," scolded Claudia, "You're infuriating at times. You haven't asked me yet."
"I knew you would say yes." said Antonio and sat down beside her.
He lifted her hand, "Will you marry me next month, Claudia?"
"Oh yes," she whispered, and she threw her arms round his neck. "How look what you've done," she whispered, "You've made my mother cry."
"She's not the only one," said Antonio softly as he wiped a tear of emotion from the corner of his eye.
Antonio later followed Dimitri into the spacious room he used as an office with its ornate, carved doors.
"Here, let's sit over here. Brandy?" said Dimitri.
Antonio took the glass and drank half of the fiery liquid before he sat down Dimitri Ferolla was an imposing man, quietly authoritative, who did not suffer fools gladly. He was also very powerful, and Antonio knew that Dimitri could destroy him at a whim if he so chose. So, Dimitri surprised him when he began.
"I like you, Antonio. You have spirit. We can work together, but your Grandfather, Mario is being pig-headed."
Antonio smiled wryly, "Don't I know it. I had one hell of a row with him before I came down here."
"Families should not be at each other's throats. Mario is a proud man, and from what my own father says, he's had to fight hard for everything he has. I don't want to

What Price Ambition?

do battle with him. We can work together, if only he would sit round the table and work out the problems. I was hoping that you could persuade him, Antonio, but now I'm not so sure."
Antonio heard the slight hint of fear of the Agusta power in Dimitri's brief statement. Dimitri knew that a fight with Mario could bring them both down, and he would rather avoid it if there was another way.
"You mean because I'm not his true Grandson." said Antonio, choosing to take the more personal innuendo.
Dimitri smiled, "I knew you were a sharp young man. Yes, exactly that. I don't know how much influence you have on Mario right now."
Antonio bristled at his casual words. Dimitri had assumed a lot. If he had influence it would not necessarily be to Dimitri's advantage.
"Influence has never been a word I would use, but my feelings for Mario haven't changed. Grandpa knows that." he emphasised the bond he still felt for Mario.
"Good, then, that's a start. We'll work on him together. Your father came to see me. He's been more than generous to my wife, his sister. It's a strange world, Antonio."
"Yes, isn't it just, "smiled Antonio, "But that's what makes it so exciting. You never know what's round the corner, Do you mind if I take Claudia out for a picnic tomorrow? The weather looks as if it's going to hold."

What Price Ambition?

"Don't ask me, Antonio," laughed Dimitri, "I'm just her father."
"I promised to deliver something for Grandpa," said Antonio when he arrived to pick up Claudia,, "But I'll do it later when I get back. It's too nice a day to waste in London. We'll go to the coast. Can we take your car? This hire car I've got is playing up. I'll drive."
They prepared the food together, and drove off in Claudia's car for the hour's drive to the coast.
"Have you noticed a problem with your brakes?" said Antonio, "They feel a bit spongy."
"No, is it dangerous?"
"Could be if they pack up. Better get them checked tomorrow."
They continued along the coastal road chatting and listening to CD's on the car player.
"It's pretty along here," said Claudia, "Just look at the sea sparkling. What's wrong, Antonio?"
She had turned her head to look at Antonio as she spoke, and she saw his face contorted and anxious. Claudia looked at the road when he did not answer her, and she saw that car was gathering speed down the gradient.
"What's wrong, Antonio?" she said again in panic.
"Shit!" said Antonio as he wrenched the steering wheel, "It's the brakes. I've got no brakes at all. Hold on, Claudia."

What Price Ambition?

Claudia gripped the seat, unable to voice the scream in her throat because of the terror which was gripping her. The car gathered speed, and Antonio crashed the lever into a low gear to slow it down, the sudden change in momentum made the tyres screech and the car jerked wildly into the road side.

It was a small country road along the cliff-top with hardly any traffic on it, and there was no-one to see the car lurch through the fence into the narrow strip about ten feet from the cliff edge. There was a drop from the road, and the car plummeted downwards, coming to a standstill with a bump.

Antonio banged his head on the mirror, and for a few minutes, he was dazed. When he came to, the car was stationary, embedded up to its sills in the mud. The engine was still running, and he turned the ignition key to switch it off. He looked across at Claudia. She lay with her head to one side against the seat.

"Claudia! Sweetheart are you alright?" but Claudia did not answer him.

Panic gripped him as he felt for the pulse in her neck. She was alive, and Antonio expelled his breath in relief. He turned her head towards him and saw the bruise on her forehead where she had banged her head. She must have been knocked out by the blow. He reached for the mobile phone on the dashboard, and in his anxiety, he pressed the first number. It was the Agusta emergency line which was continuously manned.

What Price Ambition?

"Sorry," he said, "I need an ambulance. Claudia's hurt. Oh, It's Antonio Agusta here. Yes, I'm with Claudia Ferolla. Where are we? I don't know. Near Southampton, I'll take a look and call you back."
The man on duty called Mario at once. He had flown to London on business with Nick Derwent, and he hired a helicopter to fly to the area immediately. Before he left. Mario called Derwent.
"If you've screwed up again, Derwent I'll have your hide, Antonio was with that girl. Get down there. I'll join you as soon as I can."
In the meantime, Antonio had climbed up the bank to the road and walked a few hundred yards to a road sign. He phoned the control centre and told them what it said and they said they would arrange help for him.
He paced up and down, every few minutes checking that Claudia was still breathing, and he was almost in a panic when a car arrived some twenty minutes later. He ran to the bottom of the slope.
"Where's the ambulance. Claudia needs an ambulance."
The man who had got out of the car straightened up, and Antonio stopped in surprise.
"Derwent!"
"What are you doing here, Agusta? You're supposed to be on an errand for the Don."
"I changed my mind. What business is it of yours anyway, Derwent?"

What Price Ambition?

"You weren't supposed to be in the car. She was supposed to be driving it herself. She had an appointment at the hairdresser."
Antonio's muscles went rigid as if someone had just given him an electric shock.
"What did you say?" he said quietly.
"We were supposed to make it look like an accident,"
Antonio clenched his fists, but he forced himself to stand still.
"On whose orders?" he said and held his breath.
"The Don, your Grandfather, of course. Who the hell do you think?"
"You bastard!" said Antonio and lunged at Derwent, "I'll kill you, Derwent!" he shouted, "You and that bastard, Mario."
Nicholas Derwent laughed, "I don't think so, but come on if you fancy your chances. It's just the excuse I need. Grandpa isn't here to protect you now."
Antonio swung at him, but Derwent laughed and ducked.
"You'll have to do better than that." laughed Derwent, and Antonio hit him on the chin.
"Like that, you mean?"
"Fuck you!" said Derwent, and he was just about to retaliate when the humming noise of rotary blades interrupted the summer day.
"Cool it, Derwent," said the other man, "The Don is here."

What Price Ambition?

Mario emerged from the chopper and Antonio ran towards him in a rage.
"You've done it this time. You've gone too far this time, Grandpa."
"Is she dead?" said Mario, ignoring Antonio's outburst.
"No Sir. She's just unconscious."
"Finish it," said Mario shortly, as he looked into the car at Claudia without so much as a glimmer of compassion.
"No! Leave her alone, Grandpa. I love her."
Mario turned to look at Antonio, and the sun reflecting on the sea over his shoulder, gave his Romany features a dark and sinister look.
"Please, Grandpa," pleaded Antonio, "Don't hurt her. I'll take her away. I'll get out of your life. Kill me if you have to kill someone, but please don't hurt her."
He struggled as Derwent's companion held his arm, but Mario just stared at him as if he was looking through him.
"Do it, Nick, and bring Antonio to the chopper."
He started to walk away, and with a cry of rage, Antonio wrenched his arm free, and ran at Mario. He knocked him with his shoulder in the chest like the rugby player he was, and Mario tottered backwards, taken by surprise and winded by the attack. He fell heavily and rolled down the grassy slope, slippery with the recent rain. Antonio stopped in his tracks and

What Price Ambition?

watched in horror as if in slow motion Mario rolled over the edge. He clutched at a tuft
of grass and he hung for a few seconds motionless as if time had stopped.
Antonio moved swiftly to the edge.
"Antonio," Mario whispered, "Help me Antonio."
Antonio bent to reach out to his Grandfather, and then he stopped inches from Mario's face, closing the fingers he had been holding out.
"You bastard!" he spat at him and watched without moving as Mario's old hands lost their grip. He slid slowly over the edge, his body gathering speed and bouncing off the rocks like a rag doll till it lay still and crumpled some two hundred feet below.
Antonio stared at the inert form of his Grandfather till the silence was broken by a seagull, disturbed from its nesting place by the commotion. He drew himself up with an effort, and turned round to face the other two men.
"Okay, Derwent, we can assume that Mario Agusta is dead. Get that helicopter out of here. Pay for his silence. I'm going to phone for an ambulance now. It was an accident. My car went off the road, and I phoned Grandpa to come and fetch us. He slipped while he was trying to help Claudia. Do you understand?"
"You let him die, Agusta."
"Cool it, Pal," said his companion, "He's the new Don."
Antonio straightened his shoulders.

What Price Ambition?

"Take his advice, Derwent. I am the Don, and you'd better not forget it. I don't like you, and I know the feeling is mutual, but you can be useful to me. If you're going to stay, I need your full support. Do you hear what I'm saying?"

Derwent did not move for a second, and then he stepped forward, and took Antonio's hand where he wore the gold ring with the Agusta crest. He kissed the ring and hugged Antonio in the briefest of embraces on either cheek.

"I understand. You won't get any hassle from me, Don Antonio, I know where my bread is buttered."

"Good. Now let's get that ambulance."

The police and ambulance arrived and Claudia and Antonio were taken to hospital, Mario's body was later recovered by a coastguard helicopter, and Antonio arranged for it to be taken back to Glasgow for the funeral.

He stood by the coffin as people he hardly knew filed past, each one bowing his head, both in respect for Mario and deference to Antonio. There were family, friends and all the heads of the Cosa Nostra come to pay their respects to one of their own. They had also come to publically acknowledge Antonio as Mario's successor.

What Price Ambition?

Antonio stood stiffly, his head high, unsmiling but polite and respectful to the elder statesmen of the various families who greeted him.
When the procession came to an end, and they had a few minutes before the coffin was removed, he glanced at his Grandmother who stood at his side.
She felt his gaze and smiled slightly.
"It's done, Antonio. The key is yours. Use it wisely to unlock the treasures of life. Your Grandfather's murder has been avenged at last."
Antonio glanced across the room to where Claudia stood with her mother and father, and his heart filled with love for her. She would never know what he had done for her, for the only person he had told was his Grandmother.
"Yes, I'm Don, Nonna, and you have your wish. Mario is dead, and I inherit from him. It's as it was then. I too became ruthless when it was something I wanted. I'm no better than Mario. Who's going to avenge Mario's death? Should I watch *my* back from now on?"
He glanced round the room, "Mario had sons of his own blood. Maybe they will fight his cause."
Anna shook her head, "They don't know, Antonio. It doesn't concern them. Mario didn't think it was necessary for them to know, and your father won't say anything. He always takes the line of least resistance. You promise me that you won't breathe a word of what

really happened to anyone else. You can trust Derwent, can't you?"
Antonio nodded as a family member offered condolences.
"But they must know about the Andresi fortune, Nonna. It made the papers."
"As far as they're concerned, Giorgio inherited it indirectly. Even the papers do not know the truth. The Andresi lawyers were very clever. Only the Ferolla Family knows, and they won't say anything either."
Antonio looked over at Claudia again, and she smiled at him when he caught her eye. Just for a second, he returned her silent look of love, and then he resumed the strong, impassive look of a man heavily burdened with the load he was carrying.
He pulled back his shoulders. It was a heavy load, but one he could easily bear if he shifted the weight so that it was evenly distributed. These were his people, his family, and he would pull then together into a powerful force, just as Mario had done. He had already got Ferolla under control without the man even suspecting his intentions. So, it was no different now. To be Don of the family and the extended family he planned to incorporate in the business, he would need to be ruthless, and he had realised in the last few days that he had no problems with it. He would do what was necessary. The word of the Agusta Family would continue to be honoured as before. He *was* an Agusta

What Price Ambition?

by accident of birth. Mario Agusta *was* the Grandfather he had loved, the Grandfather from whom he had learned the ways of his special world, and for whom he was mourning today. Mario would not blame him for the decision he had made back there at the cliff. Mario would have known that there was no choice for him. Mario, of all people, would understand.
Later, as the coffin was lowered into its last resting place, and Antonio stood by his father's side to throw a single red rose in with it, a shaft of sunlight broke free from behind the heavy grey clouds which had dominated the skies all day. It rested on the brass plate at the head of the coffin, and danced around the ornate mouldings. Antonio watched fascinated as its shadows seemed to be trying to form something. He tilted his head to one side, and almost jumped when abruptly the motion stopped. Clearly visible was the outline of a key, just for a second, and Antonio shifted uneasily. Maybe he had imagined it, but no, there it was again. He smiled. Mario Agusta *did* understand, and he had sent a sign of forgiveness to Antonio. Now he could see what had always been his destiny, and he was silently happy with that thought, and with his Grandfather's blessing.

From the union of the three families he had an indomitable influence. An embryo would grow, and a

What Price Ambition?

new empire would pass on to his son in time. That was the way of it.

What Price Ambition?

Other books by DD Hall

The Daggers Series…

See over for other books…

What Price Ambition?

Thrillers…

Printed in Poland
by Amazon Fulfillment
Poland Sp. z o.o., Wrocław